The Matrix Interviews

The Matrix Interviews

Moosehead Anthology #8
Edited by R.E.N. Allen & Angela Carr

LIVRES
DC
BOOKS

Moosehead Anthology #8
The Matrix Interviews, © 2001

Edited by R.E.N. Allen and Angela Carr
Design by conundrum press

Printed in bound in Canada

Canadian Cataloguing in Publication Data

Moosehead anthology

Annual.
"A collection of contemporary writing edited by the staff of the Moosehead review".
ISSN 0842-1765
ISBN 0-919688-86-1 (8th issue)

    1. Canadian literature (English) — 20th century — Periodicals. 2.
Literature, Modern — 20th century — Periodicals.

PS8233.M66 1988-   C810'.8'0054   C89-039024-X

The Canada Council | Le Conseil des Arts
for the Arts | du Canada

DC Books gratefully acknowledges the
support of The Canada Council for the Arts
and of SODEC for our publishing program.

DC Books / Livres DC
C.P. 662, 950 rue Decarie
Montreal, Quebec
H4L 4V9, Canada

Distributed by General Distribution Services through the Literary Press Group.

Contents

The Matrix Interviews, 1975-2000

An intertwined history binds *Matrix* and *The Moosehead Anthology*. In one of the periodic flourishings of English language literary culture in Quebec, both appeared in the province's Eastern Townships: *Matrix* in 1975 and the original *Moosehead Review* in 1977. Both moved to Montreal eventually, and the *Moosehead Review* became an annual (or sometimes bi-annual) release from DC Books — another variant of the literary stock, begun in the 1960s by Louis Dudek and revived a quarter century later. Now these three converge to produce a selection of the *Matrix* interviews, which began in the early days of the journal and quickly became a tradition.

In all there are 36 *Matrix* interviews, and counting. When we went back to see what was there, a pretty impressive list of writers emerged: Martin Amis, Anne Carson, Marie-Claire Blais, Amitav Ghosh, Neil Bissoondath, Gail Scott, D. G. Jones, Stephanie Bolster, Irving Layton, David Solway, Erin Mouré, Michael Crummey, Mordecai Richler, and many others. In many cases too the interviewer was a writer, and reflects the writer's as much as the scholar's perspective. Whether Mary di Michele interviewing Anne Carson, P. Scott Lawrence interviewing Neil Bissoondath, Terence Byrnes interviewing David Fennario, Carmine Starnino interviewing Michael Harris and Erin Mouré, Victor Coleman and Lynn Donaghue interviewing Michael Crummey or Taien Ng-Chan interviewing Stephanie Bolster, there is quite often a sense that it's a kind of mutual interrogation — two writers talking, while we listen.

Not all interviewers are novelists or poets. One of the best is Philip Lanthier, the original editor of *Matrix*, who did perhaps more than anyone to establish the *Matrix* interview and is here represented by interviews with D. G. Jones and Robert Allen. Brent Bambury, who interviewed Martin Amis, and Elaine Kalman Naves, who talked to Marie-Claire Blais, have reputations primarily as journalists. Robert Majzels was interviewed by Lianne Moyes, a professor of language and literature at l'Université de Montréal.

Most of the interviews follow the classic form, but for an approach of uncommon originality look at Taien Ng-Chan's whimsical three-part interview of Stephanie Bolster, and Corey Frost's discourse with Gail Scott. Then there are the interviews in which there's a sense that two sensibilities are staking out their own ground: see Carmine Starnino's interview of Erin Mouré and Terry Byrnes' interview of fellow citizen of Verdun, David Fennario. Andy Brown's interview of Nick Bantock, writer and illustrator, turns on a discussion of the graphic art of stamp design.

It's probably redundant, in this age of instant access to literary sites on the web, to try to sketch writer biographies here, so we haven't. (To quote Anne Carson interviewed by Mary Di Michele: "I am not interested in biographical data. 'Today is most of the time,' as Gertrude Stein said.") Look at the end of the book, however, for a selective listing of publications by the writers interviewed here.

Irving Layton

Interviewed by **Tom Henighan**

Tom Henighan: *One of your main themes of recent years is the Jewish-Christian relationship. We have now an attempt on the part of many Christians to heal the breach with the Jews by facing the fact that much of their hatred stems from the notion that the Jews were responsible for the death of Christ. Do you think that if Christians really deal with that unconscious, or half-conscious, belief, that anti-Semitism could be finally obliterated?*

Irving Layton: I wish I could believe that. No. I wrote a poem called "The Crucifixion," which I recited on the first program of *The Jesus Trial* on the CBC. I think there's a deeper problem here. I believe that civilization produces for the most part discontented, miserable, unhappy, lonely, alienated human beings, and such human beings, because they are unhappy, must be destructive and sadistic. Cruelty is related to their discontentment. I was amused in reading about the Guyana cult that there was a call for the FBI to investigate other such religious cults. It doesn't occur to anyone to investigate the society that produces the need for those cults. Now, I'm trained to be a scientist, and I like to look at the causes. I'm not interested in symptoms. I want to know what causes acne or indigestion, and I want to know what produces cults to which lonely, and unhappy, and lost people will surrender their individuality, their own will, for a feeling of belonging, of fellowship, however pseudo and false and glittering it might be. These things throw light on fascism, they throw light on great success, the charismatic success of a tyrant and a very sick man like Hitler, or the success of Bolshevism. I think we've got to go very deeply into this business of what our civilization's all about. So to come back to the point that you raise — if you're going to have unhappy people, they'll pick on anyone that's weak. The Jews have been weak, and therefore they've been picked on. When the blacks were weak, they were picked on. My answer is: let there be equality of power. That's the only way you'll prevent that kind of vengeance, or *ressentiment*.

TH: *To come back to the causes of the present wave of dubious religious cults.*

One of the reasons that might be given for these outbreaks is that modern society has lost its cohesion, that the great myths no longer seem relevant. Do you think people like believing Jews are shielded from existential terror by their group cohesion, the sense of the family tradition, and so on? These have been elements in your poetry, I believe.

IL: There has been this atomizing which has come about because of the industrial revolution and many other factors. The individual is very much alone, the traditional props like family and church and synagogue have been broken, and the individual confronts a universe he finds increasingly terrifying, and out of terror and loneliness he looks for other souls who are as terrified as he is. So what you have are porcupines coming together with their needles pressing together. It's a bad scene. For myself certainly my Jewishness has helped. There's a strong family tradition. Belief I do not have; I'm not an orthodox Jew. I renounced that kind of Judaism by the time I was thirteen years old: I'm an atheist. I stopped believing in a good man out there when I was thirteen or fourteen and my dear cat died in a fire. I couldn't understand why God would want to kill my cat. I could understand him wanting to kill people — because I'd seen some very nasty people — but my cat hadn't done any harm except to an occasional mouse and she was there just to do that. So I didn't see the justice of it. From then on, I think, I've been a very happy, cheerful atheist, and nothing I've seen on this planet in the way of massacres, of volcanic eruptions, floods, and so on, has in any way helped to change my mind about this idea of a deity who's supposed to be concerned with us. In fact, I've arrived at a solution for the problem of evil, for the question of why about ninety percent of all human beings live in such desperate circumstances. We are the progeny of Satan, of the devil, and God is afraid that Satan's progeny are taking over, and will perhaps spread their wickedness to other galaxies. I understand he's got a planet in reserve, so that in case things look very bleak for him, he is going to hurl the planet into Earth and send the whole thing *smash*. That's the only way I explain evil, that someone up there's trying to eliminate the human race. Otherwise, why massacres, why wars, why bloodshed? In a single day just think of the blood that's shed on this planet between sunrise and sunset. It's very hard to hold onto your intelligence when you think about that. For me the idea of a benevolent creator who might be concerned with the welfare of human beings is utterly incomprehensible.

TH: *But even eliminating that possibility — what about the idea of the human spirit itself, and the positive things that come out in poetry and art, for example?*

IL: Well, I don't believe in deity, but I do believe in divinity. That is to say I find imagination and reason to be divine attributes. These I do hold in great reverence.

TH: *From your perspective on existence, do you think the human race will destroy itself? Don't you think this element of spirit is indestructible?*

IL: Spirit may be indestructible, but the human beings that have that spirit within them are unfortunately not indestructible. You can have an Einstein, you know, or some communist bully, some communist thug can take a Solzhenitsyn and crack his skull. That communist thug will go on living, but a Solzhenitsyn or a Brodsky will be dead. And what I have seen in the last forty of fifty years are these goons, and thugs, and louts, and bullies, and depraved monsters surviving only too well, and destroying people with sensitivity and imagination, people who have the divine light of truth in their souls. That's what gets me. And no God up there to help us. And the people of spirit too few to be able to retaliate and unfortunately not having any cannons, not having any bombs to beat the bullies back.

TH: *What about the evil in ourselves?*

IL: We have to fight it. We have to fight this desire for the power, the desire to humiliate others, for that comes from our own terror of death and is an attempt to give our lives some kind of significance beyond the insignificance of the moment. You see, Freud was wrong when he thought that the guilty thing that people were repressing was sex. He was quite wrong about that. What people repress is the fear of death and the knowledge of their insignificance. It is this that breeds sadism, cruelty and the desire to humiliate others. Freud was wrong; it is not Eros it is Thanatos that is the problem for the human race. Man is the only animal that is aware of death, the only animal that knows he's marked out for the executioner, and he simply cannot come to terms with it. So our education should not be an education for sex, but an education for the acceptance of death and our own unimportance. In the billions and billions of years, rolling ahead, what are we? My God, we're not even a speck, not even a mote. It's very hard for human beings to accept that — therefore the desire to humiliate someone else to beat to brutalize — you know, the whole sordid story. That's what we have to come to terms with. I don't see any sign that we have, but that's where the emphasis must be put.

TH: *What is the relationship between this kind of permission, or focus on death, and your work as a poet?*

IL: Well, the title of one of my recent books is *For My Neighbours in Hell*. Of course hell is obviously situated right on this planet. I'd say you create through the sulfurous fumes and the black smoke and the cries and agonies of the damned — you create a temporary haven of peace, a small island of paradise; *or* a little island of defiance, a negation, a rebellion. It isn't just a question of escape, of course. There's a tension involved, but it does lead you away from the evil and frustration I just mentioned.

TH: *Meeting you, I find in you what I've already noticed in your work — an interesting combination of passionate commitment and detachment that is tinged with urbanity. How do you see those elements functioning in your life and your work?*

IL: Well, if I weren't a Jew, if I hadn't been born a Jew, then undoubtedly I would have ended up being an A.J.M. Smith. I was saved from that fate by being born Jewish. I value wit and I value urbanity, but more than wit or urbanity I value passion. I value deep religious feeling. Wit and urbanity make a certain kind of poetry but not the highest kind of poetry. Dante, Isaiah, and no doubt Shakespeare, were not urbane. The urbane poets are always the lesser poets; they are too civilized for the human race. Now I get that kind of concern directly from my Jewish inheritance. I've said before that I'm a five thousand year old Canadian and my roots are in the Old Testament. And that gives me a perspective that goes beyond mere wit and urbanity.

TH: *You mention the creative leaven in American literature of Jewish critics like Alfred Kazin and Irving Howe, and wish Canadian literature could have more like them. Don't you think that American writers might be equally grateful for the Canadians Northrop Frye and Marshall McLuhan?*

IL: It's not quite the same thing. Americans, of course, could be grateful for Marshall McLuhan and Northrop Frye, but in a narrower sense. What I'm talking about here though is a wide-ranging cultural influence. Think of the tremendous and fundamental cultural influence of the Jews in the United States of America, where, thanks to them, the very vocabulary has undergone a subtle change. Certain words, certain patters of speech, have crept into the American language thanks to the Jews. Or take a genius in a widely influential medium, like Woody Allen. I think Woody Allen has been one of the greatest influences on the American sensibility. Right? That is what I'm talking about. I'm not talking about a narrow specialist influence, you know, in one particular field; I'm talking about a grassroots influence. I think things are dull in Canada because we don't have the Jews. The Jews who might have made it didn't stay here; they went down to the States like Saul Bellow and who knows how many others because Canada has been a WASP influence. And it's been like an iceberg has been pressing down on the Canadian spirit, so that the handful of Jews that did exist could do very little. There is a definite Jewish point of view, a Judaic point of view, that is at variance with the predominant WASP point of view. But though these things I've called attention to from time to time, nobody has taken me up on them.

TH: *Northrop Frye once wrote that you obtained your creative freedom to write the kind of poetry you wanted by creating the public mask of what a genius should be like. Is there truth in that, do you think?*

IL: I'd like to subscribe to that, you know, because it indicates that, besides being a literary historian and critic, Frye is a man of some imagination. But there's not a word of truth in it. I didn't set about deliberately to create a mask of genius, to be wild and woolly and do outrageous things, so that with my left hand, so to speak, I could write poems like "The Birth of Tragedy," "A Tall Man Executes a Jig," and so on. Not a bit of truth in that. My aim was not to mask my genius, just to reveal it.

TH: *You've sustained your creative energies over many years, and you say that you don't want to become a resigned poet but to go forward with both pitchforks blazing. What kind of advice can you give to those (not only poets) who want to release their creative energies and to sustain those energies into the later years of their lives?*

IL: I'm thinking, you see. I'm looking back to certain periods of my life when I felt that things were closing in on me. A marriage that was bad — a very bad first marriage. Before that, my family — restrictive, because my family, my mother and my father, were both very orthodox Jews. And my sisters and brothers had their own spectrum of superstitions. So. I'm thinking back now to my high school, my adolescence, and remembering the sense I had that I was not free to express the feelings and the insights that I felt were germinating inside myself and the great pain I felt. And that first marriage, the great misery that I felt for two, three or four years. And then the release. And from that I learned one important lesson, and that is you must listen to yourself, you must listen to what your own heart and soul are trying to tell you. They are monitors, they are there, they are stronger even than one's own conscience, and one hears them often when one is miserable. Misery is to the soul what a headache is to the body — it tells you you're on the wrong track. So the only thing I can say, based on my experience, is that one has to ask oneself at every point: are you happy? Are you miserable? Are you doing what you want to do? Are you expressing your deepest feelings, your innermost feelings? One should always have the feeling that one is free, that one is not being coerced. That inner feeling, for me, is the most important thing. I need to feel that society is in no way preventing me from living the kind of life that I want to live. Creativity is most likely in the individual who feels that he can do what he wants to do, when he wants to do it. Now, we're not raising the question of what he's going to do with his freedom. He may put it to ill-use, but to begin with, the individual must feel that he's not being coerced by government, or state, or family, or community, into doing something which of his own free will he would not want to do. With greater understanding of course, comes the realization that the deepest coercive restraints are not necessarily family, or community, or state, but the things within yourself, and that you have to break free of the things that are preventing you from being the free, constructive, and creative person that you want to be. So for me, freedom and creativity go hand-in-hand. In fact, they are two sides of the coin. For me the grand metaphor is God's image, in the sense that God is the creator, and man is, as far as we know, the only creative force in this universe. He's the only creative force — and every individual — *every individual* barring none, has the power to be creative in some field or another, either by drawing some pictures, or binding books, or just by the way one puts carpet on the floor. There's evidence of creativity wherever you look, and what I want to see is more of it and I want to feel that no individual is prevented from being the creative personality that God or nature wanted him to be. So in life you always have to ask yourself — are you being the creative personality that you were intended to be? If you're not, you're going to be miserable. And if you are, you're going to be happy. That for me has remained a criterion all through life. And I've done those things, I've hesitated; I've had, thank Heavens! the guts, or the wisdom to kick over those traces I felt were restraining me and preventing me from being creative, from being a poet, or a teacher, or a lover. And for me, these are the great occupations.

Irving Layton was interviewed by Ottawa novelist and teacher Tom Henighan. The interview took place both in Ottawa and at Layton's home in Niagara-on-the-Lake in 1980. It appeared in Matrix #20.

Anne Carson

Interviewed by **MARY DI MICHELE**

MARY DI MICHELE: *Your latest book,* Plainwater, *has the briefest of biographical descriptions, a single sentence: "Anne Carson lives in Canada." In an earlier collection,* Short Talks, *you are described rather elusively as a painter of volcanoes. Can you tell our readers something more about yourself?*

ANNE CARSON: I teach ancient Greek and Latin for a living. I am tallish with brown hair. I am not very interested in biographical data. "Today is most of the time," as Gertrude Stein said.

MDM: Plainwater *is described or "packaged" as an anthology of essays and poetry, yet I found it in the critical anthologies section of a large bookstore. Some works need sections entirely on their own. Is this a problem for you? For reviewers? For publishers? For bookstore clerks?*

AC: Not a problem but a question. What do "shelves" accomplish, in stores or in the mind?

MDM: *Your piece, "The Glass Essay," in* Glass, Irony and God, *has a complexity in tonal composition which is quite extraordinary. The American writer, Guy Davenport, describes it as richer than most novels. Could you comment on the relationship of poetry to prose in your writing?*

AC: In practice, the distinction between "prose" and "poetry" makes itself apparent to me gradually as I work. The two modes fade in and out of one another and at a certain point the work congeals into a form. But I am uneasy with the terms "prose" and "poetry," do not know what their distinction means any more, and have no satisfactory theory of their relation. Recently, trying to write a paper about this question, I found I could do no more than describe the smell of the distinction. I did so by analogy with that moment in the Gospel of John (12:1-8) when Mary Magdalene spills nard on Christ's feet and "the odour of ointment filled the house."

MDM: *I understand the difficulty of trying to distinguish between poetry and prose in modern writing, and your analogy is very powerful. Smell bypasses the language centre in the brain and is perhaps the closest we come to pure perception. But what of genre?*

AC: Genres are conventional. Conventions exist to be re-negotiated.

MDM: *In "Mimnermos: The Brain-Sex Paintings," you interview the 7th century BC poet Mimnermos. Is a dialogue possible for you and me now or should we wait 2700 years for somebody else to do it?*

AC: Ideally we should wait.

MDM: *What leads you to use discursive forms like the interview and the essay for poetic works? What made you choose the interview form for the Mimnermos piece?*

AC: When I was working on that, I started from a translation of a body of fragments, then added to the translation an essay, in some degree historical, explaining the background of the poet and how the fragments have come down to us. And in dealing with that historical material, I found a whole lot of what they call, in Classics, "testimonia," which means anecdotal stories about the poet or about the poem, that are passed down and aren't really regarded as credible history. But they shape our notion of who the poet was as a person. And I wanted to get that stuff in — somehow — to the reader's consciousness so that he could enjoy it also as well as the strictly historical data. So I tried to smuggle that into the interview. So the interviews are about this interstitial matter that comes down to us in semi-historical sources.

MDM: *How has your training as a classicist influenced your writing?*

AC: Classics trains grammatical rigour and attention to tone.

MDM: *What are other influences on your writing?*

AC: Paul Celan, Emily Dickinson, Fernando Pessoa, Gertrude Stein.

MDM: What in particular interests you about the writers listed above? Is it something that is common to them or something unique to each of them?

AC: Economy and devotion interest me in these writers.

In a speech, Paul Celan quoted a line that's been going around in literary-critical circles for some generations now — "Attention is the natural prayer of the soul." For Celan, that seems to be a statement about his way of creating poetry because it certainly comes from the words that he chooses and the way he puts them together. And I think that has always impressed me as an ideal. And I guess I would safely say I find that same ideal in those other writers that I named.

Economy and devotion can be just technical approaches to thinking. The larger question is, "Why think?" And I believe that a fundamental motive of thinking and making stuff ... is worship. That is, apprehension of some larger-than-oneself thing. And that is missing from a great deal of modern thought.

MDM: *Does high-tech culture interest you at all? What tools do you use for writing?*

AC: Pens, pencils, notebooks mainly.

MDM: *Terrence DesPres situates the story of Antigone as a drama at the "heart of our times," where "[the] co-opting of personal being by public force has given rise to the notion that the personal is political." In your essay, "The Gender of Sound," you describe the social construction of woman as out-sider, as another species. Would you agree with DesPres, that is, with his use of Antigone as a trope for our time?*

AC: Insofar as Antigone's rationale of action is single and simple — love for her brother — she seems to me to imply woman's role as an absolute insider, however radical that may be in any given time or place. It becomes very radical when other people value only outside things.

MDM: *French feminists like Irigaray write that woman's language is not Logos, or rational, structured language. What do you suppose woman's language is, then?*

AC: I suppose Irigaray means that woman's language, if it exists, does not consist only in Logos, i.e., it is Logos plus other things — other things by definition undefinable. She shows what the other things would be like in the way she writes. I find this writing hard to read and suspect I can learn very little from it. Clarity is very important to me. What I miss most in such writing is a concern for the activity of praise and the function of worship. These are essential to human works of language ... "Into the darkness of someone else's garden ...."

MDM: *In "The Anthropology of Water," you write: "I am not a person who feels easy talking about blood or desire. I rarely use the word woman myself .... The truth is I lived out my adolescence mainly in default of my father's favour. But I perceived I could trouble him less if I had no gender .... I made my body as hard and flat as the armour of Athena. No secrets under my skin, no telltale drops on the threshold." What is the relationship of your writing to this word "woman?" To being a woman?*

AC: A relationship of dis-ease as is suggested in the passage you quote.

MDM: *Are "feminisms" of interest to you?*

AC: Not currently. Particular females are of interest to me.

MDM: *Germaine Greer in a chapter on Sappho in her history of women poets,* Slip-shod Sibyls, *claims that Sappho is "above all things a token woman; her function is to be always the single, the only one ... the exception that proves the rule." Is this what her function is or was? How useful is Sappho as a role model for writers?*

AC: Sappho seems to me convincingly unique. I believe she thought so too.

MDM: *In your first-person narratives, men seem to be mythopoetic constructions rather than other people, unnamed except through titles like "my Cid," and "the emperor of China." Why is that?*

AC: Specific names are too rich, they unbalance the tone.

MDM: *Do you mean too concrete? Too quotidian? Too "real"? It seems to me that richness, resonance is generated by these allusive names. Tom, Dick or Harry are not so evocative. Even your American Road trip leading on the literal level to Los Angeles opens or moves through images from Chinese dynastic culture.*

AC: I did not travel with Tom, Dick or Harry. The person I did travel with, so evoked, would overwhelm the narrative texture with an influx of specific data too rich for incorporation into a verbal surface. Words after all are dead. They impersonate life vividly, but remain dead. To mix living and dead is tactless. This principle of tact is well developed in Japanese renga poetry where, for example, you can use the word "flower" in any stanza but are not permitted to use a specific flower-name but once in 53 stanzas.

MDM: *Whether language is living or dead is for me problematic. In the mouth it is alive, on the page it is technological, perhaps. The mouth is silenced by death, but words, like hair, continue to grow for a while without the author. Don't you, yourself, mix the living and the dead when you choose to interview Mimnermos?*

AC: The mixture remains a verbal artifact, not animate.

MDM: *"The Anthropology of Water," is composed of a series of first person journals/journeys or "pilgrimages," which, startlingly, give very intimate details but without the context of a story. It is, indeed, like the line you quoted from Pushkin about entering into the "darkness of someone else's garden."*
  "Details are in bad taste," you write in apparent homage to Samuel Beckett. But you proceed to offer many such details which might be described as such. For example, a paragraph beginning with "Fumigating my hemorrhoids," which might make one cry out, to quote the much quoted line from the film Pulp Fiction: *"that was more than I needed to know." How would you describe your art of storytelling? What do we need to know?*

AC: Most of my writing has been a mistake and (as you point out) tasteless. Writing draws one into indecency. I don't know why. I would retract everything if I could.

MDM: *I did not mean in any way to suggest your writing is tasteless. It seems to me that your work moves, engages, through its dissonances: the rarified intellect, meditations on ideas and literary texts, along with naked flashes of the body, "the little burning red backside like a baboon." What struck me about the passages I'm referring to in the question above is how unstable the irony is.*

AC: —

MDM: *What has been the critical response to your work?*

AC: Positive, so far as I know, but I admit I cannot stand reading reviews of my work (I skim) or in general sentences in which I appear as "she."

MDM: *What interests you in contemporary writing?*

AC: Experiments, seeing how much can be left out and still make sense.

MDM: *What are you working on now? What do you project or hope to accomplish in your future writing?*

AC: A novel in verse about a red monster.

MDM: *What question might you ask yourself?*

AC: But this is your interview, is it not?

Anne Carson was interviewed by Montreal poet Mary di Michele for Matrix *#49, the cover of which features a Carson volcano painting.*

Erin Mouré

Interviewed by **CARMINE STARNINO**

CARMINE STARNINO: *Nicole Brossard once said that there can be a great risk of "change[ing] your style of life, your perspective on reality, your relation, not only with people but also with literature, history, science ...." Were you yourself ever scared by that risk?*

ERIN MOURÉ: I think that there is, in some people's eyes, a risk in being identified as a feminist because there is still all kinds of anti-feminist discourse around us. But I don't have any problem in identifying myself as a feminist. And I think that hasn't limited in any way what I write about or how I approach things. I think there's more of a risk in not being who you are. I would have been scared not to take the risk.

CS: *You're obviously aware of the debates that surround your books. Why do you think that some people regard your work with so much skepticism?*

EM: I don't know. Because it's different? I guess I think of myself as an explorer, and so I'm not necessarily that interested in some people's discomfort, or in the kind of debates that the work evokes in some circles.

I think, however, that while such people may have read some of my poetry, they haven't read other work that would provide a context for it. And so, the poems might seem strange, or disconnected in some way, or puzzling. But I do think it's healthy to have debate around the work. If it evokes debate, it's because people are curious.

CS: *Is there something about the nature of your exploration that makes some people feel uncomfortable?*

EM: Part of what I'm interested in is disrupting conventional notions of reading and conventional notions of how we dramatize our experience. Also, problematizing the notion of "experience" — the idea that you can reproduce experience, that you can represent it exactly in words, that language is a transparent medium that doesn't bear with it certain cultural constructs.

13

My primary interest lies in the area of how the brain works and processes information. How do we know what information is? How does the brain receive it and how does what I know about the brain refract upon and affect what my possibilities are for dealing with anything in language?

I look at all of this as a feminist, as somebody who says that there are a lot of social and economic structures that don't allow women to position themselves as subjects and to speak. To me, language is just a material that's limited by the constructs and suppositions around it. But if you can unbalance those a bit, language becomes limitless. I'm in favor of finding new ways of being able to look at things and structure things, so that everybody has a chance to speak.

CS: *In reading through "The Acts," — the short essays that appear at the end of* Furious *— I got a sense of the theoretical concerns that shape your work. As I understand it, language determines not only how we explain our perceptions to ourselves and to others, but also constructs what we see. How exactly does the brain fit into that?*

EM: There's no pure, unmediated perception. What you see is identified to you by the circuits in the brain or the maps of neurons. And there's no place in the brain where everything is already put together, in the sense of a complete picture. There's no little reproduction of the outside world inside the head. There's just this big sampling process going on, and connections being made. What the brain will do, though, is it will only recognize what it already knows.

In tests where someone is shown a drawing with a smudge over the letter "r," the brain will try to identify that as the letter "r," or the letter "b." It will be puzzled, but eventually it comes to a decision or a small range of decisions about what it's seeing. Even if information is missing it glides right over it. Another example. In the eyes there are no receptors for sight where the optic nerve is; that's what's called the blind spot. We don't see the blind spot when we look because while there is missing information the brain samples from the information close by and fills that gap. Wherever there's information that's incongruent with the other samples, it will eliminate it.

CS: *So what does that have to say about how we perceive and interpret the world?*

EM: That we are in grave danger of seeing too little with our conventional structures. It means that we have to question our own structures of interpretation and structures of belief and perception. And one of the ways that I question that is to make language refract off itself in different ways, be it through words, or parts of speech, or grammar. I find it a very interesting process, and the works of others, like Norma Cole, Harryette Mullen, Leslie Scalapino, Myung Mikin, and Lisa Robertson — just to name a few of the poets I've been reading these past weeks — are great company. I'm not the only one doing these things; I am still only learning.

CS: *How does refracting language allow you to question those conventional structures?*

EM: It breaks down usual reading habits, the usual structures of what can be said. It opens ambiguities, contradictions, paradoxes that allow more information to be present, available.

CS: *Is it possible that your perception of yourself as a lesbian and your perception of yourself as a feminist are both products of the same structures of interpretation and belief that the rest of us have absorbed?*

EM: Of course it would be. That's why it's important to continually call things into question. I mean, all of sexuality is constructed. It doesn't matter whether you're heterosexual or lesbian: it's all constructed in the same way, and can turn very compartmentalized unless people are willing to call those structures into question. Where do they come from? Who are they serving? Are they giving people space to speak, and be, and grow? A chance to experience the world more fully? I don't think we have any of the answers to these things but what we do have is some tools for doing that questioning or exploring. And I also think that no one writer — although it's not just writers who are doing this but also the people in all of the arts and in the scientific fields — that there's no one person who can use all the tools.

My own contribution is, of necessity, limited. No one work or one person's writing or one approach is going to give us a complete sense of things. To me, what's important is having space, so that writing becomes a community of endeavour.

CS: *But if what you say about perception is true, what does that say about your work?*

EM: I don't think you can ever get out of the process, or get completely out of the construct. In 1988, I gave a talk at the feminist book fair saying that the margins rely on the centre to be the margins. The two terms work together. In

Parallelogramme, in 1994, I believe, there was an art critique by Vancouver poet Lisa Robertson saying it's time we questioned this whole discourse of the margin and who this whole discourse is serving. Because when people are positioning themselves on the margins, then they're inside the same structure: they valorize themselves and their choices without necessarily changing the structure at all.

CS: *Are you frustrated by that?*

EM: I wouldn't say so. I mean, it's something that you just have to discuss in new ways, using different angles, so that you don't end up stuck in the same kinds of oppositions.

CS: *What do you look for in poetry, or, more specifically, in other people's poetry?*

EM: I look for work that challenges me but that isn't just randomly all over the place. I can recognize when someone is using a more conventional form very beautifully and I can appreciate that. But it doesn't stimulate and challenge me as much as some other work would. I look for someone who's challenging assumptions about language and not just absorbing all the stuff that we've already read somewhere else and spitting it out again. Someone who's trying to move that exploration into another space. And, at the same time, I like the confluence of personal and private space in the work; that isn't just personal. I like density and urgency, too.

CS: *Emily Dickinson said, "It's a poem if it makes you feel as though your head were taken off," and for Robert Fitzgerald, poetry is "chiefly hair-raising." How do you experience poetry?*

EM: I don't know if I would be able to put it that way. I mean, some of the "hair-raising" stuff is concocted; it's as banal a manipulation of people's emotions as Hollywood cinema. Even so, I understand what Dickinson and Fitzgerald are saying. I think my response would be to say — and I thought of this, just a little while ago, when you were talking about me being scared — to say I'm scared all the time when I'm writing poetry! I'm always thinking to myself, "Whoa, where did that come from?"

CS: *Is it an emotional release?*

EM: It's not a release, but an entry. I just get into this totally wondrous state.

CS: *That fear you just mentioned. What kind of fear is it, exactly?*

EM: Fear of not knowing how I'm going to deal with what I'm doing or how I'm going to keep the process open. If I start to write a good line, or if I get some good bits, I get anxious about whether I'll be able to keep the process open and keep going.

CS: *Is it fear of failing?*

EM: Of not being capable, yes. Of not being quite capable and then losing it; using old tricks to "contain" what is opened up.

CS: *You've argued that accessibility is just a way of talking down to people. Why?*

EM: There are lots of reasons and places for accessibility. I have said before that 'accessibility' is sometimes just used as a stick to beat people. That's my problem with it. I mean, it's useful in a newspaper, but it can be a reduction in poetry because once you state something — one image, or one thing — you're making a choice and eliminating a lot of other formulations or openings. Much in the way that the brain chooses certain parts of sampled data in order to construct what you will see, and the rest of it gets left out. I think that some of what gets left out in the so-called 'accessible' structures are things that do have emotional power and force, that do have constructive force, and that's what I want to access.

When I say that accessibility is a stick sometimes used to beat people, it's because there are some people who believe that the conventional means have to be the only adequate ones. We're taught, or most people are taught, one way of reading or grasping information, and it's really useful if you're going to read the newspaper or read the ads and be a consumer, which is, in some sense, your true role in this society. And the way we learn to read helps us consume. But there's different ways of reading and of approaching different kinds of work. And I think people, in order to appreciate them, have to have the chance to learn those different ways of reading.

You'll see a lot more innovative or questioning work in places where this is possible. The Kootenay School of Writing in Vancouver, and magazines like *Raddle Moon* and *Writing*, have helped create a context. Once the context exists, then people's ideas start to open up in a very exciting way.

CS: *What's the alternative to accessibility?*

EM: I don't know if you can look at it like that. Once you learn how to work with or deal with different types of work, they are accessible to you.

CS: *But I've always thought of accessibility as something that circumvents any closed society of writers like the Kootenay School and allows everybody to have access. Given the importance of what you're trying to say, don't you want to put the poems in the intellectual reach of as many people as possible?*

EM: But isn't it "closed" to insist there is no access when the access might just be different. I think that people have a great desire to grasp new things. And that many readers do like work that challenges them. Some people tell me. "Erin, if you wrote like *Wanted Alive*, more people would buy your books." But this isn't true. In fact, my most accessible book is the one that sold less. So it's patently not true. I know there are people who like that book. But I don't always have to keep doing it. And I think poetry is a form where people do look for more exploration — and then go to the sports page to get the other stuff.

CS: *You once said, "I feel sometimes … that I'm writing other people's poems, as if fulfilling a responsibility towards them. Artists are focal points for ordinary people." Does that still hold true? There are some extremely difficult poems in* WSW *and in* Sheepish Beauty, Civilian Love. *And I have a hard time thinking of those poems as "focal points for ordinary people."*

EM: I came to a point where I realized that I couldn't project my experience of witnessing somebody else's experience onto them in poetry: that I couldn't write 'for' anybody else. I came very quickly to the point where that remark wasn't a very workable thing for me.

CS: *That reminds me of "Seebe," your long poem that derives from your experience of riding in a train that hit a little boy. You say something near the end of "Seebe" that I find very startling: "The writer as witness, speaking the stories, is a lie, a liberal bourgeois lie. Because the speech is the writer's speech, and each word of the writer robs the witnessed of their own voice, muting them." Do you really believe that?*

EM: Yes. It is in some senses true, and it is the danger inherent in the idea of "witness." In writing "Seebe," I realized that I could not possibly be evoking the little boy's experience of the accident.

I can remember bringing this little boy into the train and he'd never been in a train in his life. Just being in there and seeing his response to the train — a place that I lived and worked, a very ordinary kind of environment — I realized that he could have just as well been going to outer space. There was no way that I had access to any of his experience of the world. This was a little boy from a different culture, from the country, and one who lived on the Stoney Indian reserve at Morley. This is where we hit him. He was just out there fishing like other people, but on the railway bridge, which wasn't a good idea. And thinking back and seeing his look I understood that I had no way of entering his experience. The end of the poem "Seebe" wasn't planned. I was writing and I suddenly realized that this was unworkable. My version of the experience was sealing over his. I mean, I still think it's important for people to witness crimes and tell us what they can about them. I just don't think that, as a writer, I can "represent" somebody else's "experience." Since then even my representations of my own are suspect.

CS: *Part of the identity of your poems is their reluctance to conclude. Your poems seem to need this reluctance, need this suspicion of closure. Why?*

EM: I've managed to learn ways to resist the desire to close everything up into a neat package, to insist that the thought process be completed. I have the willingness now to let things stay open or to try and see where it's going before I figure out how it's going to coalesce. And not just depend, for guidance, on the one or two techniques that I learned earlier in my career. I think our conventional notions about what coalesces and what a finished thing is prevent us sometimes from seeing everything. When you move out of the more conventional notions, there are fewer recognizable markers at first. I think I've learned to trust letting go of those things. Like letting go of the edge of the pool to swim.

CS: *But closure and openness are relative terms. Even the most radically open texts have closure, since they're closing off certain possibilities of meaning by raising others. In that sense, what distinguishes closed work from open work?*

EM: Open work allows for more exploration, more resonance; it places weight on other meaningful levels or aspects of language — like sound, for example — rather than just placing weight on the denotative aspect. It allows more ways of having parts of things refract, more ways of creating working structures. I think it's quite possible that in fifty years what I'm writing now may be considered to be closed forms. Because I think what we talk about in terms of closed forms are forms where we understand all the points of reference: "Yes, now the poem is finished and this is what ties it up." It's a comfortable way to write something out. And open forms are forms where the points of reference are more tentative.

Scientists don't repeat the experiments of Einstein, and no one expects them to (in fact, quite the opposite), but it doesn't make them any less glad that Einstein was there. Whatever domain you're in, the most interesting thing is to try and push forward into the unknown.

CS: *"Barrington" is one of my favorite poems of yours. The poem enters deeply into an event and slowly lures the story out, detail by detail. In your more recent poems however, there's an aggression, a strategy of interposing images and lines with an interval of white space which reminds me, physically, of ruptures. What was it that lead you to replace the gracefulness of your early work with something far more disruptive?*

EM: In the same way that openness and closure can be interpreted from various angles, gracefulness and disruption can as well. But I think that I just became more interested in how different parts or segments might refract off each other and how one segment can influence how you feel about another one that went earlier. I just became interested in looking at structures and perception in a different way. I like "Barrington" as a poem, too. I put it in my *Selected*. But I felt that I had exhausted that avenue and that approach. I think that rupture is also a form of structure. I think it's more reassuring to read a poem like "Barrington" than "The Jewel," but reassurance is no longer what I'm seeking.

CS: *The poetry that I appreciate most is the poetry that, however disquieting, is able to accommodate me. What's the value, for you, of not reassuring a reader?*

EM: I like confronting discomforts, I guess. The text produces them and the reader has their own way of sorting that out. Rather than sort it out for the reader, I just trust them to sort it out. It's just one set of approaches.

CS: *In a poem like "Barrington," I can imagine the process of revision because I can clearly see the care with which you've shaped the poem. But in "The Jewel," I have a much harder time imagining the process because so much of the poem seems arbitrary in its effect and in its intention.*

EM: One of the things that's become important to me is that there's not just the connotative or denotative value of words. That's not the only thing that you're working with because sounds evoke other sounds. A word reminds you of another word. So, it's a process of trying to produce a lot of echoes. I work revising lines, changing words, because you change one word and it changes the whole piece.

CS: *What makes that different from the revision process in a poem like "Barrington?"*

EM: Because I'll now change a word to something that doesn't make any conventional sense in the context, just to see what it will do, and what it will produce. And then I might change something back. And I love doing this. I played with a poem recently where I changed the word 'beautiful' to the word 'tentative.' In the end I changed it back, but the effect was amazing. It helped me look at the whole piece differently.

CS: *I do get the sense sometimes that I'm meant to experience the poems as "a series of rhythms" — borrowing T.S. Eliot's phrase — rather than something cognitive.*

EM: I think that that level — the "series of rhythms" level — is just as important to me as the cognitive level. It produces all these reverberations and effects that are a different form of cognition, in a sense. They amuse me and I have fun and they make me feel happy, so I do them.

CS: *Do you have anything to say about your new book,* Search Procedures, *which will be out this spring from Anansi?*

EM: *Search Procedures* carries on my explorations from *Sheepish Beauty, Civilian Love.* I'm still working with the notions of poetic difficulty I've tried to speak of. But also, in the work, are hope, joy, loss, longing, desire, sexual presence, wonder. What is a person, after all, but a "search procedure?" In the book, I deal with the notions of instability of any location and the effects of that on what a person is, on how we can think, and communicate, and love. All of this work is, in the end, about love anyway.

Montreal poet Carmine Starnino interviewed Erin Mouré in Montreal in 1996. It appeared in Matrix #47.

Stephanie Bolster

Interviewed by **TAIEN NG-CHAN**

THE WRITERLY INTERVIEW

TAIEN NG-CHAN: *Is there a particular way that a poem tends to come to you?*

STEPHANIE BOLSTER: There isn't one way that it always happens, but if I'm writing nature poems — which I do often — a certain phrase will come into my mind, so it's very much the words that are the starting point ... whereas with the Alice poems, it would be something really interesting that I would read that didn't let go of me, and it would keep coming back. And I often didn't write the poems then, it would be months later. But I think my process has changed, it used to be much more that I could sit down at the computer and say okay, I'm going to write something, and something would just happen, and maybe it was worth keeping and maybe it wasn't, but now I'm much more deliberate.

TNC: *In that everything you write has to fit into a book?*

SB: Yes, although I don't think it has to be that way. The League of Canadian Poets has a listserve discussion group, and there's been this discussion in the last couple of days about putting a manuscript together, and some people were saying why is it that editors are pushing for a book of poems rather than just a collection of individual poems, and do people necessarily want to read that — should writers be trying to force connections that aren't really there within the poems. But I just like working with a theme, I guess, or certain subject matter, partly because I'm always envious of people who can write novels — they can come back to work and they have something ongoing that they're doing, so I like to create projects for myself in that way.

TNC: *How did the Alice poems start? I remember you were working on them a long time ago at UBC, maybe almost ten years?*

SB: Yes, I think the very first poems I wrote about Alice were about the same time we were taking that class with Keith [Maillard], I think it was '89/'90.

TNC: *I remember you back then saying you had an interest in fairy tales ...*

SB: I was taking a class in the English department on children's literature, and I was taking a poetry class with Daphne Marlatt. We had to do a chapbook, and I wrote a chapbook from the point of view of female characters in fairy tales, like Snow White, Cinderella, and then I started doing some stuff from Peter Pan, and then I did Alice ... Alice was the one who stayed there after I finished that project. I wrote some more Alice poems and it started there. I really didn't start thinking about it as the beginnings of a book until I started the Master's program in '92. So it was 5 or 6 years that I was working on it as a book.

TNC: *You've published a lot of Alice poems that aren't in the book ... how many didn't make it in?*

SB: Probably as many as did make it in, maybe even more.

TNC: *What was the process of selection?*

SB: It was reaaally long! Because my thesis, the way it was structured, had five sections, it had a very organic quality to it, I think. It sort of moved in and out of our world, the world of Wonderland, the world of the real Alice, it had a kind of spiraling in and out movement to it.

TNC: *Why didn't you stick with that in the published version?*

SB: I think it was because I worked with a lot of different people on this man-uscript, and some didn't know how to approach it, this mingling. They said they couldn't see the intricate connections that to me seemed very clear, they said why do you have this poem about Alice as her husband's dying and this poem about Alice after he dies — why are they in different sections of the book, why don't you build this narrative because it's already there, why are you deliberately breaking this up? And I couldn't really come up with a clear reason other than that somehow I didn't want it to be a closed system and a clear narrative. Then I thought, well, what would happen if I made it very clear? Here is Alice's childhood, and here is Alice's adulthood. And by doing that, it sort of felt like I was losing something, because a lot of the poems didn't fit any more, but it also made it seem much more like a book that you could read through from beginning to end. And it also let those connections resonate throughout the poems instead of pulling them apart. So in the end I was happy with the way I structured it. Most of the poems that I took out, I look at them now and I still like them, but I see why I didn't keep them.

TNC: *You've been widely published and I've seen a lot of your work around, yet you had a hard time finding a publisher for the book. Why do you think that was?*

SB: I don't know! It's not that I was expecting that someone would publish it right away, but I thought that the fact that I could list all these periodicals I've been published in, that that would make a difference.

TNC: *Yes, I heard at that time — I guess it was about three years ago — you'd just had your 99th poem published!*

SB: Yeah…! Well, one press did specifically tell me that I should just take the strongest Alice poems and make them a section within another book, and they thought that readers would become impatient with a book that was just Alice poems. I seriously considered that, because workshop members had occasionally suggested the same thing. For a while I thought, I don't even want to publish this — it felt like I'd outgrown it and I was working on new stuff … but then I thought, no, it's worth it, so I kept sending it around and finally Michael [Harris] took it. So I was really glad that I didn't give up on it.

TNC: *What's next for you?*

SB: Well, I have a new book of poems that was basically written simultaneously with the Alice manuscript … it was just known as the "non-Alice poems." It's called *Two Bowls of Milk* and it's much less closely linked. There is a thematic arc that goes through the whole thing but it's more loosely connected as a book. It's more of a series of sections that are linked: one is a series of paintings by Jean-Paul Lemieux, and then there's a series about different artworks in the National Gallery, so there's a lot of stuff that's inspired by visual art in that book, about half of the book. It's never really about the art, but more of a way of exploring ideas. And then there were a lot of poems written while I was still living in Vancouver, and poems about moving to this very different place, and my whole connection with landscape and family and why I still feel so rooted there but living apart from it. So it's much more overtly personal than the Alice poems — it's the way I'm writing now. I mean, the Alice poems, some of them are very old, but with this book the older poems got thrown out along the way, so it's closer to who I am now.

THE ACADEMIC INTERVIEW

TNC: *Martin Gardner, in the intro to* The Annotated Alice *(London: Penguin Books, 1960) points out that "the Alice books lend themselves readily to any type of symbolic interpretation — political, metaphysical, or Freudian."* What kind of symbolic interpretation are you most fond of?*

SB: Well, I've dipped into all of them, but the political is probably the least interesting to me, in the sense that he intended politics then, as a very direct commentary on certain political leaders.

TNC: *Like the White Knight is meant to be so and so ...*

SB: Yeah, and a lot of that came out in the illustrations, the way certain characters were drawn, because Tenniel was a political cartoonist as well. He was known for that. The metaphysical was something that interested me a lot at first when I was writing the poems, the idea of what is actually real and who dreamed it. You know the very last chapter of *Through the Looking Glass* is called "Which Dreamed It," and initially, at the end of the book, I had one page that in the middle said "Which Dreamed It" — the idea of questioning if this was the poet's dream, was it Dodgson's dream, was it Lewis Carroll's dream and what was the difference between them. So all those questions of reality and dream and identity, all of that is something that interested me. Obviously, there's the Freudian thing which can't be overlooked. I had some early poems that were very parodic about the symbolism of the rabbit hole and all those kinds of things. Just the idea of going underground — that's where the Alice and Persephone poem came from — it's just such a potent symbol that you can't not notice it.

TNC: *The poem "Portrait of Alice, Annotated," is obviously a comment on textual analysis. Can one read Alice now without a sense of its annotations/history? Do you feel Alice has been over-annotated?*

SB: I have really mixed feelings about it, because at the same time that I find

---

* p 8, where the following quote is also found: "Consider, for example, the scene in which Alice seizes the end of the White King's pencil and begins scribbling for him."

it's very constraining — it makes us look at everything historically instead of just enjoying it the way it was intended to be read — I was fascinated by how densely layered it is and how much it was written very much for a particular audience, with all sorts of political in-jokes that we would never get now. If you know anything about Alice and Lewis Carroll, you know there's this speculation about their relationship, and because she's so much of an icon, people have expectations about the book. It has that weight of history, just like any classic text. You can't get beyond that.

TNC: *As you say, there has been much speculation about Charles Dodgson and his "interest" in little girls in general, though many sources painstakingly point out that while he may have been "in love" with Alice Liddell, there was "not the slightest evidence" for him committing any "improprieties," that he thought his passion quite innocent. In your book, you made a choice to portray Dodgson's attentions to Alice as clearly sexual. Why did you make this choice and what influenced you to do so?*

SB: I don't think of it as being clearly sexual, but with very clear sexual undertones. I don't think I could come out one way or another and say whether something actual happened, because that's something that can't be known. I've read those same books which say it's unfair of us, which it is, to read it by our own cultural norms when it was such an entirely different time... and when he would take pictures of nude little girls, there were always chaperones there so that it would appear appropriate. But at the same time, I read about these crises of faith that Dodgson would have, waking up at four in the morning and writing all these things in his journal about not being good enough, it just made me think that, well, I don't think he himself understood what was going on, but there was something that troubled him about what he was doing. Also, letters he would write to mothers, apologizing for having kissed their daughters, or whatever ... it was something like, he protests too much, type of thing. And the photographs I have seen — there were four that survived — they're very disturbing to look at .... When I saw them I thought there's definitely something going on here, regardless of what he or Alice understood of it. I couldn't not address that in writing these poems.

THE SURREALIST INTERVIEW

Lewis Carroll was interested in psychic phenomena and automatic writing. Playing on this, the interview was conducted in the following way: As automatically as possible, I would write a question on a scrap of paper, fold it over, and hand it to Stephanie, who, without seeing the question, would write down an answer. Here are some of the results.

TNC: *Who are you?*

SB: What's left after the winter goes.

TNC: *Where is the sky?*

SB: I understand what you're asking, but only the water knows.

TNC: *For what use are looks?*

SB: Because fascination goes nowhere: the secret is in the proximity to the thing.

TNC: *What is a hand?*

SB: Three things: the hourglass, the smooth stone, and the empty room.

TNC: *When do you wake and why?*

SB: Kafka knows the answer best; don't ask me.

THE WRITER BEHIND THE BOOK INTERVIEW

TNC: *What's your favorite colour?*

SB: Green! I actually have an office now that's sort of a pistachio green.

TNC: *What's your sign?*

SB: Libra ... which is meaningful in certain ways, in the sense that it's all about balance. I always feel like my life and my writing are trying find balance between making money and having time to write. I guess it's more about being a writer than being a Libra, but it's something I always think about.

TNC: *Have you always been a writer? When did you start writing?*

SB: Yeah, I've always written, even as a little kid, I'd make up stories and stuff.

Poetry I sort of wrote when I was 13 or 14. I wrote poems about whatever teen idols I was obsessed with at the time.

TNC: *Like who??*

SB: Duran Duran. Don't out me as a Duran Duran fan ....

TNC: *I don't know, it's far too tempting! Though I'll admit I went through a Duran Duran phase too, at 13 or 14.*

SB: And I still have those poems! In shoeboxes somewhere ... but I think it was when I was 16 that I read Sylvia Plath for the first time, who is a terrible role model, but I really connected with her poetry, and that's when I really started writing poetry.

TNC: *That's such a teenage cliché!*

SB: I know! But I really thought at the time that I was the only person on the planet — I actually wrote a poem about that but I never published it anywhere — about that feeling that you're the only one to experience this, only to find out years later that all kinds of teenage girls were reading Sylvia Plath! But that was a beginning point where I started writing more seriously and I didn't really stop after that.

TNC: *How's life been since you won the [Governor General's Prize]?*

SB: Life's busy! And I am busier now, but I know that's a temporary thing. I guess the good thing is that I'm getting asked to do things instead of having to ask to do things, like readings. I still feel really lucky to have won, but you know, it is so arbitrary, I think that had it been three different people on the jury, had the jury met on a different day, who knows, it could have easily been someone else. Ultimately it just affirms what I've always thought, which is that writing the stuff, the good moments of writing are really still the most gratifying moments. If it's possible in any way to make a living through piecing all these things together, then that makes it easier. But I'll still make the sacrifices I have to make to be writing.

Matrix *contributing editor Taien Ng-Chan interviewed Stephanie Bolster in Ottawa in 1998, where she then lived and worked. It appeared in* Matrix #54.

Michael Harris

Interviewed by **CARMINE STARNINO**

CARMINE STARNINO: *What, in a word, is at the root of your work?*

MICHAEL HARRIS: Mortality — and the quality of joy that comes from having to come to terms with mortality. Sex and Death. Creation and destruction. In a word, 'nature'. When I see those qualities manifest themselves in an event, or ceremony, or in an habitual act, then I think it's my job as a poet to remind people, and myself, of those respective impulses. Take the idea of survival. As a primal impulse it's interesting. If the colonels come in and decimate a village, for example, I understand that there are other villages springing up three hundred miles away feeding off the fat of the people who were victorious in the slaughter. That's how history seems to have gone: certain people wipe out other people and some people seem to profit. It's a matter of accepting the notion that that's what being human is. Now, I'm not saying that it's greedy or evil or good. I'm just saying that, as a poet, I recognize that the impulse is there. I wish with all my heart that the world were a peaceful place. But it's not, and I can't pretend it is. As an aside, I'm in the middle of Norman Davis' *History of Europe* — an extraordinary book, and one that takes a very unsentimental look at the multifoliate horrors humans seem capable of.

CS: *Do you think that politics has any place in poetry?*

MH: Absolutely. If actual politics is woven into the fabric of normal human affairs in a day-to-day way then obviously it has to be taken into account. Much of Seamus Heaney's work reflects that predicament — his poem "Casualty" is a good case in point. But at this point in Canada, in my daily life, I tend to write about what I know. Apart from what the newspapers report, I don't know a lot about what's going on in, say, Uganda. I could imagine it, but I would prefer the Ugandan poets do that — that's their job. I listen to Yehuda Amichai about the Israeli wars. I listen to Mohammed al-Maghut about Lebanon. I read Akhmatova and Mandelstam about — well, you get the point. I don't think it's possible to write in the twentieth century without understanding that more people have been killed in this century than in all the other centuries combined — more viciously, and more effectively. But the birds still sing, the crows fly, the snow falls. Not to suggest that those subjects are more worthy of poetic attention, but they're not in the realm of parochial political thinking. I think that politics, and how we view social interactions, are very much like the dance of light on the waves curling over the sea — only it's really the sea that I'm interested in, and not the dazzles of light that attract one's eye. They're there for a reason: they're there because much larger and more powerful forces put them there. I can understand how one can get caught up in local or national or even global politics, but I don't really see them as things in and of themselves, as behaviours in and of themselves. I see them as reflections of other, more primal impulses. And it's my perspective that those impulses are the stuff of poetry.

CS: *So you've never felt the need to opine on a political situation?*

MH: Not as such. It's very seductive — facile, really — to pontificate on the morality of political situations. It's easy to say, for example, that the British should remove themselves from Ireland, or, equally, that the Orangemen should protect their turf. But the problem with a lot of politics — and poetry that has, at its heart, an evangelical message — is that often both sides have cases to make. And there are real human beings on both sides of the fence — or rather, on all sides of all fences. I'm more interested in common denominators than the fractions they produce. Poetry, for me, is a matter of clear sight. I don't write poetry to render judgement on a situation or make the world a better place. If the forest is burned down in order to produce lumber for some greedy land baron in the Amazon, and a species of butterfly dies, I regret that, but that seems to be the way of the world. I'm not suggesting that I don't feel it should be stopped. It should indeed, if we can manage to do so humanely. What I am drawn to is the very fact that it happens.

CS: *Would you call that perspective fatalistic?*

MH: I don't think it's a matter of being fatalistic. It's a matter of being realistic. Poetry is like a memorial speech given at a funeral service. The best memorial speeches are always the ones which, in fact, are closest to the truth. It would be ideal if, even then, we could tell more truth than we do. But we tend to live a kind of euphemistic life, and while we all have our coded ways of expressing what the truth is, it's very hard to be so forthright that in being that forthright one can still be socially acceptable. Anybody who's obliged to an employer, or a family, or a religion, or a political idea, will find it very difficult to subjugate themselves to the idea of truth-telling, if, in fact, they still want to be on the social playing field. Shakespeare came pretty close, I would say. And didn't lose his head. Many did: Lorca, Mandelstam — the list is very long. But, if possible, it might be more productive to be a working saint than a defunct martyr.

CS: *As a poet, how do you see your responsibility to your community?*

MH: I would like very much to be an outsider, in all possible respects. The notion of the poet for me has always been that of the solitary: the person who has isolated himself for whatever reason and reports on that situation via poetry. It's a difficulty for me that I can't be solitary enough. I find myself occasionally paralyzed because I can't get far enough outside the obligations and demands of myself as a father, or a teacher, or an editor, or whatever else I do. So my responsibilities to my community are met, but they're not poetic ones. The poetic one is to be alert to whatever happens in my immediate sphere. And that's the material I write about.

CS: *Let me ask the probably unanswerable: what exactly do you write about?*

MH: I imagine that like every other human being I'm unique in the sense that I've had an unshared experience of the world, and that's what I write about. I am, in other words, the book with which I am most familiar. But in the soap opera of my life — getting married, witnessing death, having children — auto-biography is just a source of information, in the same way that other people's lives, or other poets' works, are also sources of information. If I live a conscious life, the thing I'm most conscious of is myself. Through the knowledge that that consciousness brings I filter all other experience. Of course, I do hope that, like the ideal journalist, I can set aside that explored conscious self such that I can see other selves for what they are and for how they define themselves. But the Confucian edict is that one looks into one's own heart and the heart of one's family to understand truth, and so ultimately it is the inward turning eye that produces the most significant verse.

CS: *Did your years of teaching mean anything to you as a poet?*

MH: Teaching underlined the fact that, as a writer, I had an audience and that audience was a very receptive and responsive thing. It didn't feed me as a poet to teach; although I suppose by osmosis the more I taught, the more I learned, and I tried to teach new poets every year, so I possibly benefited that way. But it was much more nourishing, for example, to be in the middle of a Greek island and be the poet without apparent restriction. I find that the work I've felt most pleased with has taken shape in places other than the city or, in particular, the school.

CS: *Do you really think the academic life is liable to block a writer's sensitivity to his own intuitions?*

MH: The academic life makes one conservative, as would working in any institution, I imagine. Not so much because you're trapped in it, due to financial obligations, but simply because there's a behavioural matrix under which every teacher must function, and, for a poet, that can cause a kind of behavioural shadow to sometimes fall over the work. There are obviously enough instances of good writers who have gotten on with their work in very domestic, inglorious situations. I think of Borges the librarian, Larkin the librarian, Eliot the banker, Stevens the insurance man. But institutions are nonetheless democratic places, and I think the poet, essentially, is a very undemocratic sort of person. I think that's the attitude from which most good poetry comes. It's often anti-conventional, sometimes anti-social, or, at least, asocial.

CS: *There is an aspect to your poetry which sometimes strikes me as — to use a shopworn and probably inaccurate word — cathartic. I'm thinking here about "Turning Out the Light," the long poem about your brother's death, and how, throughout it, you subject yourself to an often excoriating self-investigation.*

MH: If there's a distinction between art and life, the distinction — although also arbitrary — is a temporal one: an event takes place and the poem takes place at a later date. In other words, one takes the time to work the poem such that the flavor of the actual event is represented truly. So it's not an investigation of myself as such. It's a matter of trying to achieve an effect to allow the reader to see what I saw then, and what I see now. Of course, I can't say that I don't meet little personal revelations along the way, or that even after I finish a piece I don't encounter more still. But you're suggesting that my poems are cathartic for me, and what I want to suggest is that a great deal of my life is absolutely mysterious to me. Things are so rich! How can one intellectually manage the ten thousand events that inform one particular episode? I mean, at best a poem can deal with maybe four or five. The impulse behind "Turning Out the Light" was that I experienced something that I wanted other people to experience. So I wrote the poem in order to achieve that particular effect — not to say, again, that I'm unaffected myself by the poem when I've finally done it. I get drawn into the spirit of it as much as any other listener. But I don't consider that cathartic or therapeutic because I'm working to achieve that effect in the listener.

CS: *Can you explain what you mean by the "arbitrary" distinction between art and life?*

MH: The idea I feel very close to at this time is not so much that beauty is truth, or truth beauty, but that art very much is life and not something distinct from life. For years I had the sense of some ordering principle that would have me be outside of nature, even of my own nature. That the best I could do was observe it, look at it, and try to learn from it. And what came to me in my third book, *Grace*, was that there's no distinction between me and nature, between what my world is and what I see. The visionary landscape is the thing that in fact we live in. Emily Dickinson in "Death and Miss Emily" is a little dispossessed of nature because she's trying to connect with it in dozens of ways — everything from making jam to examining how bees work. And her own vision, and the vision of the poem, comes when she realizes that all of the animals, all of these primal energies, are in a kind of wedding procession. The dowry of which has to do with her death. So, in other words, her vision is that with life comes death, and that she is not at all separate from what she had previously observed — as an onlooker.

CS: *How are your recent circus poems different from your previous work?*

MH: If there has been a change in my work over the last fifteen years it's been from a kind of verbal density on the page, rich in images, to something more colloquial and simple. Initially it was a matter of identifying, in as spectacularly clear a method as possible, whatever it was I was looking at. If I were looking at a porcupine I would want it to be so bristly on the page that you could feel it. And now what I want is the spirit of porcupine to be accessible. I think what I'm trying to do is make it so simple that, as in Ted Hughes' "Thought-fox," the animal "appears" on the page because the reader puts it there. I should add that if my language has become more simple, there's also a new whimsy about it. Whatever it was I felt dark and complex about in my twenties and thirties I now seem to colour with humor. Perhaps as I get older, and my time grows shorter, I feel there is no better reaction to life than laughter, or at least a grin at the whole thing.

CS: *Do you think you're beginning to take yourself less seriously?*

MH: Rather than take myself less seriously, the whimsy is one way of dealing with something that is deadly serious. "The Confectioner" — one of my newer circus poems — is, despite its seeming insousiance, ultimately about the complicity of the 'writer-persona' in the realm of cataclysmic historical events. Thus, in a poem like that, laughter becomes merely another form of baring one's teeth.

CS: *I assume your expectations of poetry have undergone some concomitant change as well?*

MH: My love of language hasn't changed. I still enjoy it for its own sake. I have, however, become a much tougher reader. I'm now much too weary of pretension. I like the idea of poetry that does honour to the canon, that furthers the poetic enterprise.

CS: *How would you characterize your contribution to the poetic enterprise?*

MH: When I take a hard look at something, I try to get the gist of it right, try to get the essence of it correctly. I try not to lie to myself or veil the work in euphemism, inappropriate insights, or misjudgements. What I want very much is to see things straight and clear, and to survive that information, whatever it is, with equanimity.

Carmine Starnino interviewed Michael Harris in Montreal for Matrix #55.

D. G. Jones

Interviewed by **Philip Lanthier**

Philip Lanthier: *You've recently retired from the University of Sherbrooke's Department of English. How has it been for poetry? Do poetry and retirement go together?*

D. G. Jones: At certain periods of the year. It's a problem sitting down and finding something to say; one ends up talking simply about the weather, or talking to yourself as it were, keeping your hand in. I have a series of poems from when I was in St. Martin's in the winter. I reread them recently and I think they're interesting enough to publish.

PJL: *I've noticed, reading through your last book of poems,* The Floating Garden, *that the world beyond North Hatley is very much there: an earthquake in San Francisco, Palestinian refugees, the Intifada. You seem to be tuned to the surrounding world.*

DGJ: That's the other window. The television is one window and the windows in the house and studio are another. The two are there all the time; it depends on which is likely to bore you first. The news gets pretty depressing, but you digest it as much as you can and occasionally something strikes you.

PJL: *One of your poems in* The Floating Garden *struck me in particular,* "Fin de Siècle *Springtime Ramble." You write of "the world conceived as wreckage." What kind of wreckage?*

DGJ: Well every spring there's wreckage. We see the wreckage from last season, especially when the lake overflows into the park. There's a great mess out there that someone's going to have to clean up. But every year, every generation, every century has its wreckage, some of which is physical, some of which is emotional and intellectual. We do very well in terms of wreckage.

PJL: *What do you mean by intellectual wreckage?*

DGJ: Certain ideas and values that we arrive at which undergo a certain amount of damage from year to year, generation to generation. Certain absolutes, social or religious. Our present moment is filled with wreckage from the 50s and the period following World War II when people thought that things were booming, that we had it made, that we're going to have a stable society and be able to afford all kinds of nice social programs. We thought we had a stable economy too, but all that's gone out the window.

PJL: *The economy, or "the climate of investment" as you put it, is a recurring theme in* The Floating Garden. *You've turned your attention to economic wreckage.*

DGJ: "Christmas/Going on" gets into that idea. Why the death of two ordinary girls who lay down on the railway tracks and were killed should have grabbed my attention I'm not quite sure, but for some reason it did.

I suppose it focused certain convictions that everything was changing. There was also anger at a world which is often blithe in its moral assurances and social conventions. This kind of event shakes that assurance. What I saw happening in the world around us because of global changes in economics has been described in Angus Reid's book *Shakedown*. Capitalism in particular is really shaking up, and shaking down established business and social institutions. With the whole East becoming prosperous, the West is being put in jeopardy compared to the easy life it used to have before. As everybody rushes in desperation to compete all kinds of things go out the window.

PJL: *Including the two teenage girls who "missed it," as the poem says.*

DGJ: Whatever these girls had as a problem, they missed getting involved in the human community.

PJL: *Did you have floating Japanese gardens in mind with the title?*

DGJ: I offered other titles but nobody liked them. The editor, Chris Dewdney, suggested *The Floating Garden*. It comes from a phrase in one of the poems where everything is breaking down and drifting away. It's an image of an order that is continually breaking down, being recreated, and floating. It does have echoes with the Japanese floating world, but that's not exactly what we get in this book.

PJL: *You spoke a moment back about writing at certain times of year. Many* *of your poems are autumnal, Novemberish. Has this got something to do with a* fin de siècle *feeling?*

DGJ: That certainly goes with it. The time when you hole up in your study and write tends to be winter and fall, though fall is one of the more stimulating seasons for me. This summer I had a batch of translations to do and to get other people to do, so that took my mind off writing other things except occasionally. There are a number of poems in the book that are done in linked series over a month or so. This is one of the things I wanted to do after I retired, sitting down with a rough theme and doing a poem every day or two and going on until I had 7 or 13 or 21 or whatever.

PJL: *The poet David Solway complained a number of years ago that the language of Canadian poetry is too transparent, too watered down, too colloquial and has therefore "forfeited the power to move," and more recently, the novelist Charles Foran complained of the "neutral" aspect of Canadian writing in English, though he excepts Anglo writing in Montreal, and writing from Newfoundland. English Canadian writing strikes him as on the whole "bland," lacking the "uninhibited, cocky, endlessly protean" quality of Québec French. What would your assessments of these comments be?*

DGJ: I remember reading the Foran article. Most English Canadian writing and speech in public contexts is pretty tame compared to Newfoundland and the kind of Québec French you get on comedy programs. He's probably right in certain areas, but whether this is true in the case of poetry I'm not so sure. There's more of the colloquial idiom in some of the French poetry of the last twenty years as I've found out in preparing this anthology. Certainly the speech in the poetry of mid-century and before was not colloquial at all, though rich enough in metaphor. You begin to see that change in the work of Gaston Miron in the 60s in what he called the "*non-poème*," not that his poems look "*non-poème*-ish" these days. No, a lot of [Canadian] poetry is not particularly interesting from the point of view of the liveliness of the language. In *The Floating Garden* I was trying to let the language become a little wilder.

PJL: *But don't you think poets like Peter Van Toorn are pushing the limits of language, poems like "Mountain Boogie," for example?*

O peonies! the flutes of spice!
O spinach wrinkles!

O fire chopping a log to strips of ash!
O yoghurt thwop!
O clam-shell tulip-cheeks!
O pink-spoggled eggs on umber craterboard!
O saffron velleity!
O opal winter lightning through the onyx glass!
O bamboo arpeggio!

DGJ: It's taken a while but Van Toorn's poems have finally been recognized as interesting stuff. But it's true that not too many poets have played around with language. The poetry is in the play of language and not simply in representation or bearing witness. A lot of Canadian poetry is fairly descriptive and biographical. It's about family and especially nowadays about mothers and grandmothers, a new wave of the same old thing, but the way of seeing and experiencing has not changed much. To alter the language is to alter the way you think and feel. You feel according to the conventions of the language you inherit.

PJL: *Doesn't it get back to the old problem of Canadian identity? Unless we can find a language with distinctive characteristics, which poets can help to create, we find ourselves swallowed linguistically by the Americans?*

DGJ: You can't legislate this collectively. It happens or it doesn't happen collectively. The Americans are all over the place — in the South, West, New England — but they don't all speak in the same way. We do the same thing from the Maritimes to B.C. but it's not so obvious. And it's not because of John Crowe Ransom that the people of Atlanta talk the way they do. Poets don't determine the way people talk; it's up to the people themselves to be inventive with the language. In that respect, the Québécois, especially the last generation, have had a ball with their language, especially in the media of radio and television. People complain about it being silly or idiotic, but it's been extraordinarily inventive, using old and new words, puns and neologisms. Some of the ads are zany and some are just plain stupid. They don't mind risking being stupid. English Canadians are shyer of pretending to be stupid.

PJL: *Which may be a defining characteristic of the rest of Canada?*

DGJ: We want to be cool.

PJL: *A recent poem of yours, "Excerpts from Daily Wallpaper, a Book of*

Samples" appeared in Matrix *a few issues back. Are you composing on the computer screen? Is it changing your poetic line? Your poetic language?*

DGJ: Yes. That poem started as I was playing around with various font sizes and typefaces. I was using stuff out of the news and putting it all together the way, as McLuhan says, you put together the pages of a newspaper, a bit of this and a bit of that, with presumably some kind of unity, at least for the day, to suggest a certain excitement. I did a whole series and published a good part of it in Matrix. I also suggested it for *The Floating Garden* but the editor said no, most of it's dated. He was probably right. But he wanted to take the line from Nancy Sinatra's song out too.

PJL: *"These boots were made for walking?" He didn't think people would catch it?*

DGJ: Well I wasn't sure whether he thought people wouldn't catch it or whether they would. I must say that was one of the better lines in the poem.

PJL: *And one of the few songs for which Nancy Sinatra is remembered. It's odd that a line like that would be questioned when there's a reference in another poem to angels in the snow as "purdy depressions." Was Al Purdy making angels in the snow?*

DGJ: Well not exactly. He's got a poem in *Poems for All the Annettes* [1962] where the girl he made love to in the snow had left her rear end as a cast in the snow and he went back to look for it. It's a form of angel I suppose.

PJL: *The editor didn't object to that one?*

DGJ: No, but he wanted me to take out the rap bit, I'm not sure why. Maybe he thought it was politically incorrect or the appropriation of language and he would have people banging at his door. Writers borrow everything, steal everything they can. If it works, it's worth stealing.

PJL: *Immature poets borrow; mature poets steal.*

DGJ: Everybody borrows whether they're good poets, bad poets, it doesn't matter. It depends on whether something lively comes out of it. I suppose it's dangerous when you're presenting a representative character, but hell you can't go running around being politically correct otherwise you'd never say a thing. This may be an aspect of Canadian language: manners, not to tread on anyone's toes. If it works for me, I'll probably use it. Whatever comes along that opens up a possible way of talking, a rhythm, an arrangement: try it out.

One of the things I was trying to do in *The Floating Garden* was to let the world of everyday discourse — radio, television, newspapers — into the poetry, trying to open up the poetry and absorb the language of the surrounding world, to digest the verbal world of one's own time, the language of politics, commerce and science.

PJL: *Is there a danger that this language will become dated? Lose its force?*

DGJ: This is one of the dangers, but there's also the potential vitality of renewal. You split the two. John Donne in the seventeenth century made good use of the language of geometry, geography, commerce, minting money, exploration of the new found lands. The danger is you may not make good use of it, as my editor was worried I didn't.

PJL: *The digestion becomes indigestion.*

DGJ: Or it just goes flat as the clichés and popular tunes fade out. Though some of them go on and on. They're good. But up to a point it worked. Some people said "Oh yes, it sounds real, it sounds *now*," which is not often people's reaction when they read poetry.

PJL: *There's a phrase which appears from time to time in the opening poem, "touch and go," which I take it is not only a reference to the unhappy fate of the two girls but also to your poetic technique, a quick movement from item to item which often makes it quite challenging to the reader, because your poetic line is filled with puns, quick shifts, changes of rhythm, little enigmas, a quick, compact type of poetry. What is your advice to readers faced with the difficulties of your poems?*

DGJ: If you can enjoy jumping around, help yourself. If you can't, it's not for you. Many of the poems don't have a hard core coherency or theme. They try to tie things up in a glancing fashion; the ideas aren't developed logically.

PJL: *Do you see yourself writing within the imagist tradition?*

DGJ: The power of the image, the idea of locating things in an image is not foreign to me. Most Canadian writers were familiar with the imagist tradition, though the idea of reducing poetry to nothing but the image was a bit more than they were prepared to limit themselves to. I did do a thesis on Ezra Pound, but that was a long time ago, and I don't have quite the same compulsions or theories as he had.

PJL: *What about Wallace Stevens? You share a knowledge of French, of the visual arts, of the atmosphere of light? Has he been important to you?*

DGJ: He's one of the poets I can reread. He's one of the major poets of the twentieth century, one I keep referring to myself in certain poems then wiping away. There's the sheer power of his imagery and metaphors to begin with. He's also one of the most coherent poets. He kept trying to rewrite the Romantics. That whole question of the imagination as creating the world was a Romantic belief. The imagination somehow got you in contact with some kind of absolute truth, which, of course, Stevens didn't believe. All we've got is our imagination; that's the way we make up the world, but whether or not it's got anything to do with the absolute is another question. He wrote the poetry that would illustrate Northrop Frye and Frye wrote the criticism that would illustrate Wallace Stevens. Stevens was also recognizing the interest in language which characterized the 30s, 40s and 50s, the whole linguistic revolution, [anticipating] post-structuralism and its questioning of language itself, the possibility that this is a highly arbitrary and relative medium you're working with. What meanings are these? Is there any anchor? I think Stevens had a sense of this as he worked through his poetry. Unlike many great poets at mid-century he was cultivating a post-modern awareness.

PJL: *Do you see yourself as a pastoral poet?*

DGJ: Yes, but I keep making fun of the pastoral because I'm sitting here writing pastorals. I'm not quite sure what to write about these days.

PJL: *Is there a distinctive Canadian pastoral poetry to which you feel attached?*

DGJ: Well yeah. It goes back at least to Lampman, many of whose poems I can identify with. I grew up in the same kind of country and it seemed natural to read him. One of the real surprises was to read Nelligan, same time, same country, not many miles between Ottawa and Montreal. For Nelligan the natural world was of no great consequence; the important thing was the ideal world, the world of art, beauty, spirit, mind. There was also this terrible tension between the ideal and the bodily in his poetry, so he was not inclined to write about the landscape. Lampman, on the other hand, grew out of Wordsworth and the other Romantic poets. Most of us in English Canada tend to see ourselves in terms of land and space while for a long time French Canadians saw themselves in terms of language, word, realities represented by symbols or signs. This produced a wholly different kind of poetry and culture. Two peoples living at the same time and in the same place and they didn't see the world at all in the same way.

PJL: *Do you think this is a problem now, not simply a gap between two poets but between two linguistic groups?*

DGJ: The difference between French Québec and English Canada is not that great anymore. *La gloire de France* doesn't mean a damn thing to most Québécois, and all the absolutes of the Church — intellect, spirit — don't mean any more to the French Québecer than they ever did to the rest of Canada. The world shared is increasingly more substantial and it's the world of contemporary culture. In this anthology of French Canadian poetry which *Ecrits des forges* is putting out and for which I've been doing some translations, the poetry since the 60s is more popular, more individualistic. If there's a collective identity it's not political, religious, or a solid front of any kind.

PJL: *What kind of criticism of poetry do we need at the present time?*

DGJ: Any really serious criticism would be desirable. I suppose that most of it is going to be produced by academics, but as you imply there hasn't been a great deal of consequence in the last while, probably because interest in poetry has become secondary, but also because there's been a shift in the criticism itself. It's all about post-colonial literature and women's literature.

PJL: *Do you think this interest is misdirected?*

DGJ: I think it's boring. After a decade or two of great complaints about thematic criticism, that's exactly what we've got: large generalizations and themes that gather all kinds of stuff together.

PJL: *So what kind of criticism do we need at this juncture?*

DGJ: Almost anything that brings an informed awareness to the reading of individual texts and authors. D.M.R. Bentley's *Canadian Poetry* used to promote something called "ecological criticism." That seemed to be a confusion of postmodern ideas and familiar to Canadian concerns with space and place; it seemed to imply that cities produced sonnets and the Canadian Shield produced epics. Some of his more recent articles, like the one that illuminates the relation between Carman's poetics and late nineteenth century ideas, half-medical, half psychology, on "nerves" in modern life, seem more properly concerned with the "ecology" of literature.

PJL: It sounds like a pretty traditional form of criticism.

DGJ: Yes, the comparatists call it the history of ideas. The new criticism doesn't replace many traditional approaches; it merely complicates them. Despite suggestions to the contrary, the questions of genres, forms, prosody even, their relation to the institutions, literary or non-literary, of their time remain of real interest. The new criticism only makes it harder to take some of the ideas for granted — that epics are superior to cookbooks, that the claims of a canon are self-evident, that absolute verities spring from the mouths of poets.

PJL: *Your neighbour, poet Ralph Gustafson, died a little over a year ago. Would you care to comment on his contribution to the Canadian literary scene?*

DGJ: It's obviously been fairly large. A kind of miracle, in fact. People made a great thing of his first Penguin anthology [1942] and I don't want to diminish that at all. The idea that he was putting Canadian poetry into the pockets of Canadian soldiers and sending it around the world was apparently real enough. He was known almost exclusively for this for many years until he came back to Canada and bought a house here in North Hatley. His career as a Canadian poet really begins with *Rocky Mountain Poems* [1960] and after that the number of books he published was extraordinary. He used to complain that he wasn't getting enough attention, but to get so many books published year after year, to receive awards and to get readings all over the place — I thought he was having a remarkable career. He was also writing himself into a Canadian tradition of poetry, making his own distinctive contribution to it, giving us a poetry of place, of civil order, of civil life, and of intimacy with one's locale, which was especially striking for a man who traveled so widely and who wrote so often about exotic places. For the most part I prefer the local poetry and think that's where the strength is. Some of his wit, vocabulary, turns of phrase, come from the general sophistication of his life and produce poems slightly different from the local ones. It seems to me that Gustafson really did produce a body of work which gave Canadian poetry a breadth, intensity and particularity which wasn't there before. He became a major Canadian poet under people's noses, without their knowing it.

PJL: *What influences has Taoism had on your writing?*

DGJ: I am in no sense a practicing Taoist, but it has had a profound effect in certain ways. What's struck me is that its basic view is that of the twentieth century semioticians.

PJL: *You'd better explain that.*

DGJ: Well, there is a kind of analogy between them. Lao Tsu begins by saying that the tao that can be told is not the eternal tao. That is the nameless. The named, however, is the mother of the ten thousand things, like heaven and earth, night and day, male and female. These, however, as symbolized in the yin/yang are relative, and the opposites may change places. Night becomes day, wet dry, good bad, male female.

From Saussure and Morris to Derrida, the argument develops that all languages are relative and arbitrary — differential systems for creating meaning, which we tend to consider "reality." That is, as we create more and more signs or names, we create ten thousand things, structured in terms of binary opposites and hierarchies. Canadian poets often point, a little enviously, to the Inuit with their many names for snow, a nicely discriminated "reality." Equally rich is the French vocabulary for talking about wine. One could also point to the hierarchy of angelic beings, from angels to archangels to dominions and powers, and on perhaps to the fallen angels or evil powers. That was once a defining feature of "reality," and may still be operative in certain TV series in fashion today. However, Derrida argues that language can never say anything about origins, essence or Being, about absolute reality. That tao that can be told is not the central tao.

PJL: *Does this affect the form of your poems, or is it more a framework for seeing, or perceiving the world?*

DGJ: No. In a very simple and crude way it's one point where I can implicitly or explicitly talk about silence or empty space or a rich void.

Is not the space between heaven
  and earth like a bellows?
It is empty without being

exhausted:
The more it works the more
  comes out.
Much speech leads inevitably
  to silence.
Better to hold fast to the void.

             [Lao Tsu]

Ted Blodgett [*Apostrophes*, Buschek Books, 1996] has been into silence, which is one of those paradoxical ideas which writers get interested: Silence. Haw Haw. Shut up. The paradox. I keep trying to read a book by Jacques Derrida about all the things that make language, that make meaning possible. But they seem to be things you can't put your finger on; they never really appear; they're always not there. This means the gaps, silences, aporias, nothingness, craziness, which make things possible.

PJL: *Your poems seem to rely on gaps and silences. We spoke earlier of the way images, thoughts, enigmas slide and jump over spaces. You don't build poems rhetorically.*

DGJ: More and more it's a question of leaps, a question of not getting locked in. You want to have some kind of rigor, but logical rigor or even metaphysical rigor can be so bloody boring. If you want a certain kind of demonstration of a purely logical kind then that's marvelous, it's what you asked for, getting from A to B to C to D, like how do you get your computer to work and how did they build these things in the first place. This is admirable, but at the same time you feel this terrible depression. People get locked into certain views and that's it and it's dull, and it's also so often a trap. One of the images I have of a poem and of living is broken-field running. The thing is to keep going and not fall flat on your face with whatever comes up; bumps, holes, ups and downs, winds, logs. You keep going up and over and around. You negotiate all these things and to get there you also have to digest them. That's what people do in living. That's what the modern world keeps telling you to do. You don't settle down to anything. You keep your eyes open and watch what's coming up.

Philip Lanthier lives in Lennoxville, Québec. He is the founding editor of Matrix *and the author of numerous critical articles, reviews and interviews. He interviewed poet and critic D. G. Jones in North Hatley, Québec, in 1997. It appeared in* Matrix *#50.*

Robert Allen

Interviewed by **PHILIP LANTHIER**

PHILIP LANTHIER: *Now that you're about to publish a Selected Poems with Véhicule Press of Montreal, I thought this would be an appropriate time to go back to your first two publications with Ithaca House at Cornell University. What kind of poetic atmosphere did you find yourself in at Cornell? Was there a certain kind of poetic community which got you going?*

ROBERT ALLEN: Yes, I guess there was. I'll go back a little further than you asked. I'd just come from Toronto where there was quite a fermentation going on. Dennis Lee had started Anansi Press and there was a lot happening with the new small presses. There was a group of 20 or 30 younger poets in Toronto that I was familiar with, and a few slightly older poets like Michael Ondaatje and Margaret Atwood. I started writing in that kind of context.

PJL: *A context of Canadian nationalism?*

RA: Yes. It's funny that I ended up in the States because I remember writing an extremely scathing and self-important review of some American poetry of the time, and then I ended up doing a Master of Fine Arts in creative writing at Cornell. I came back to Canada five years after that with an entirely different outlook, a little broader I guess, and probably a little less nationalistic.

PJL: *In other words, though you began to publish books of poetry in the United States, your writing career began in Toronto. Can you say more about the atmosphere there?*

RA: Well, it was pretty exciting, but I was still in University and on the periphery of things. I did put together a manuscript three or four months before I left Toronto and gave it to Dennis Lee. He was quite kind about it; in retrospect he was very kind about it. But that was the basis for *Valhalla at the OK*, which I eventually published with Ithaca House in 1971. It was pretty pretentious, very learned and larded with the sorts of things you pick up in literature courses and around poets and small presses. In Toronto I published a few poems here and

49

there in magazines, but I didn't do that much. When I got down to Cornell, I found things were very interesting and far more advanced politically than the University of Toronto had been. Things were absolutely chaotic.

PJL: *I remember visiting Cornell in the mid-sixties and finding libraries with smashed windows.*

RA: We loved it at the time We thought that was progress. Just a few months before I got there, some students had taken over the student union building with machine guns, so everything was in ferment and the whole graduate program had pretty well ceased to be anything at all except in name because the students had pressed to abolish rules and deadlines. There was no structure at all when I got there; I was told I could do anything I wanted and that's basically what I did for four years. It was wonderful. I guess it's since retrenched, but at the time there was a sense that anything could happen. This feeling was part of the writing program which had at the time pretensions to being one of the best in the States.

PJL: *Did you go on the basis of that reputation?*

RA: Well no, actually I hadn't. I'd been offered a lot of money by the Ford Foundation. I spent four years there studying literature but I knew in the back of my mind I wanted to write more than anything else. I went into the medieval studies program, which was very good at Cornell. But after I spent a year doing that, I decided it was too much for me. So I ended up in the writing program. It had been started by Baxter Hathaway, who I guess isn't a household name in writing, but who was a very good teacher and had managed to attract some very good writers and to provide a press and a magazine. I believe that *Epoch*, which is still going, was quite a high profile magazine during the 60s and early 70s They were among the first to publish Joyce Carol Oates, Don Dellilo and a number of other American novelists and poets. Some Canadian writers too. I remember discovering George McWhirter through his *Epoch* manuscripts. A.R. Ammons was at Cornell, a writer with a big national reputation, but there were others like Joanna Russ, Alison Lurie and William Matthews on the faculty.

PJL: *Did you meet these writers on a regular basis? Were they in charge of courses, for example, or was it more of a loose-knit community, especially given the unstructured nature of the graduate program?*

RA: Well, outside of one weekly workshop, it was rather unstructured. But people did get together; I recall being at houses out in the country quite a lot. The only reclusive person in the program was A.R. Ammons, who is a very private and wonderful man.

PJL: *Was any one of these poets particularly influential?*

RA: Well, Ammons primarily, and another student a couple of years ahead of me, Jerald Bullis, whom you will know from magazines. I was particularly interested in what both of them did with the longer poem. Ammons wrote poems which were 50 or 60 pages long, and so did Bullis. I've got a poem called "Voyage to the Encantadas" which goes back to Wallace Stevens, poems like his "Notes Towards a Supreme Fiction," the kind of long, loose and metaphysical poem which is more eighteenth than twentieth century. You don't see much of that in Canada right now. There are longer poems, but they tend to be different sorts of things. I'm thinking, say, of bpNichol's "Martyrology."

PJL: *Or Dennis Lee's* Civil Elegies?

RA: Yes. They're in a different tradition entirely. The American style of long poem that I came into contact with tends to be very elliptical; it changes tone a good deal and tends to ramble and meander. It's chatty and has an American, especially American Southern, kind of verbal structure: very dense and very interwoven.

PJL: *Writing a longer poem and hoping to get it published is something of an act of defiance against the trend isn't it?*

RA: If you assume that you're going to publish in magazines, it can be difficult. But more and more writers bypass magazines these days simply because they are so time consuming and pay so little and take so much effort. I remember years ago trying to make sure that every poem I published in a book had first appeared in a magazine. I picked this up in the States; it's a bad habit. At the time the book is going to press, you send everything out in a hurry.

PJL: *I know people that do that still.*

RA: Yeah, but it's got less and less that way. In my last book only four or five poems had previously appeared in magazines. I felt myself consciously writing for a book instead of sending things out to a journal. That may be because having to deal with editors and having to send your works in unasked can be a little hard on you if you're turned down flat. And the longer you write the more tender your ego gets, so you keep things back and send them out only to people who ask for them.

PJL: *The times were turbulent: the Vietnam war, black power. How did you, in writing poetry, relate to these events?*

RA: I was far more of a public and political writer than I am now, although that's probably because the political and social aspect of what I do now is worked into poems or fiction better. It doesn't stand out there all by itself. I wrote a lot of polemic things back then and I published a few of them. Most don't really stand the test of time. They were topical, but I'm still to this day trying to write a really good political poem. Being 22 or 23 years old at the time, I was consciously against a lot of traditional and accepted things in art. So I would write the poetry of statement or the poetry of shock, something that was there for everyone to see, as in Ginsberg and that group of poets.

PJL: *Did many of these poems simply get filed?*

RA: Yes, a number just didn't get published anywhere. There are a few in my first two books (*Valhalla at the OK, Blues and Ballads*). Two or three Vietnam war poems for example. But the kind of poem I ended up writing ten years later was different. There's a poem in *The Assumption of Private Lives* (1977) called "The Great Dictator" which is really a kind of social essay and is not overtly political. I've always felt uncomfortable — at least I do now — with the rhetorical, political poem. It's not that I don't believe the things I'm saying; it's just that I don't like the tone of my voice when I say them. My work is naturally reflective, so the spontaneity of political rhetoric is difficult.

PJL: *Were you giving public readings at the time? Were there public readings going on during which the political poems were being recited to suit a particular moment, and worked?*

RA: Poems wouldn't have appeared in the numbers they did had not that kind of thing existed to encourage them. I remember writing poems an hour before doing readings. Everyone did that. There was a real sense that the public production of a poem was separate from what appeared later on the page.

PJL: *A political urgency to say certain things quickly to an audience and get* *a reaction?*

RA: Sure, and nobody would bother about the stylistics. Actually, even in print people didn't bother much about the stylistics. I was lucky in that Ammons, the most influential of my teachers, was a stickler for the line and certain technical aspects of poetry that not too many people were paying a lot of attention to. They were more interested in the tone and content and political stance, and you could get away with an awful lot technically if you had those other qualities. Now, I think, if I brought poems like that to a creative writing class at Concordia in 1987, I'd face a lot of tough questions.

PJL: *Did Ammons go through some of your poems line by line with you?*

RA: He didn't work with other people's poems line by line. It was more a sense in his general criticism that every word and every line were important even when you had the sense of something flowing freely and spontaneously. He gave lectures. I remember him talking for ten or fifteen minutes just on why it's important to end a line on a certain kind of word, or begin on a certain word, or what effect you could get by doing one or the other. I hadn't really thought about that too much at the time.

PJL: *Robert Lowell is said to have done the same thing. He would take a student's poem and give a disquisition on the first line and then another on the second line, and of course the poor student was cut to ribbons.*

RA: Well, Ammons never did that. He's a very gentle man. He would not dream of cutting someone down to size over a poem. It simply wouldn't occur to him. I don't recall getting very much negative criticism from Ammons.

PJL: *So, following Cornell, you went to Kenyon.*

RA: Yeah, I taught for a year at Kenyon College [in Gambier, Ohio].

PJL: *That's another literary centre in the United States. Was the atmosphere much different there?*

RA: It was quieter there. Things had died down with the retirement of John Crowe Ransom ten years before I got there. There had been a famous summer school at Kenyon in the 40s and 50s which he had organised. But after he retired, all that went pretty well by the boards. I actually lived next to door to

Ransom in 1973-74, the last year of his life. I could see the flickering of his TV screen, and every now and then I could see his daughter, who took care of him, but I never saw him the whole year that I lived there.

PJL: *Frederick Turner wrote an introduction to* Blues and Ballads. *He was with you at Kenyon then?*

RA: Yes, actually that was what sustained me during my year there. Fred and I would get together two or three times a week and read each other what we had written. It was a very small place, but there was always the sense that you were in the middle of the Southern literary world because of Ransom's connections.

PJL: *The process you've been describing — from Toronto to Northern New York State to southern Ohio — is a drift deeper and deeper into the United States. You were in fact absorbing more and more American influences.*

RA: Yes, and it was entirely accidental too. Some of the most profound influences occurred because I just happened to pass somewhere and meet somebody. I remember when I first got back to Canada feeling a little disoriented because what I had seen as interesting five years earlier seemed not quite so interesting.

PJL: *In returning to Canada you were in a position to make comparisons and contrasts between two literary worlds.*

RA: Yes, and it was interesting too because I'd been so dismissive about a lot of American poetry while living in Canada and then turned around and got dismissive about a lot of Canadian poetry. Then I found a balance about two or three years later. But there are still aspects of Canadian poetry that I have difficulty with.

PJL: *You've written in a* Moosehead Review *article [1978] to the effect that there is essentially no Canadian avant-garde. This was a few years back mind you. You also expresses a certain disdain for the Canadian cultural establishment, particularly the Canada Council, which seems to militate against experimentation.*

RA: I found experimentation, but I thought it was on the ground already pretty well covered. I'm a little less strident now than I was ten years ago when I wrote that article. I'm not even sure it's wise to talk about an avant-garde because there are so many ways a work can be new and interesting and so many ways it can be old-fashioned and irrelevant that I don't think you can stamp it with a particular label and do it justice. I found that a lot of Canadian avant-garde poetry is based on various post-structuralist and post-modernist principles that I didn't have much sympathy with, although they're interesting in an intellectual way. It's playful and there's a certain spontaneity and immediacy about it, but it just isn't very interesting in a sustained way.

PJL: *To pick up the biographical thread here. After Kenyon you went north and east to Prince Edward Island. Why?*

RA: I was out of a job in 1974 because of immigration problems. I went with a friend of mine, Michael Farrin, who was working on a book on Wittgenstein and Marx at the time. We drove up in my old Rambler station wagon with everything we owned to what we figured would be the cheapest place to spend the winter. In retrospect, we should have gone to Mexico. It was the worst winter in decades. But we both spent eight months there and got books out of it, which was OK.

PJL: *The book you got out of it was* The Hawryliw Process. *Is that where you started it?*

RA: That's where I wrote most of it. I finished it in North Hatley two years later. I'd been working on it on and off since about 1970, but it was seventy or eighty pages of things that didn't quite fit together. It wasn't until I spent a long winter on Prince Edward Island in a farmhouse with the wind blowing around the eaves and the snow piling up to the top floor windows that I actually brought the whole thing together.

PJL: *Now this is, of course, a great potwalloper of a book. You say you began as early as 1970? I'm interested in the genesis of it, the original seed.*

RA: There were a couple of original seeds. One is that I read a couple of books — this was the summer of 1969 — that got me thinking about the structure and shape of novels in a way I hadn't done before. One was *At Swim-Two-Birds* by Flann O'Brien, which is still one of my favourite books. In its initial drafts, *Hawryliw* was formally influenced by that book primarily. One night at a party I wrote the first twenty or thirty pages. That may be an index of the party or of my state of mind at the time. It was in a big house in Rosedale, so I was able to withdraw into someone's study.

PJL: A big house in Rosedale. Did that become the model for the Hawryliw Institute?

RA: There may have been a few details worked in. I had no clear idea of the novel at the time. Even now, fifteen years later, I still believe that writing a novel should be organic; it ought to accrete gradually. Any novel that I'm going to write is going to have to be structured like that unless it's a short thriller, or novella. I found that I wanted to write about ideas and you can't have ideas out of the blue and just write about them, or at least I can't. Writing that book I stumbled around a lot and played around with ideas, many discarded since, and it wasn't until about two-thirds of the way through that I finally got a half-clear notion of what I was trying to do.

PJL: *So the novel itself was a process of discovery, an investigation into the world of ideas.*

RA: That, incidentally, is why I like the long poem so much, because it gives me the opportunity to let my ideas and observations work themselves out. I've found that just day to day life is grist enough. If you've got some ideas, some concepts and generalisations and basic directions, then everything that happens, everything you see or talk about can be incorporated as you go along. That's something that Ammons taught me, that there was no matter too slight or too irrelevant or too extraneous to be brought into a certain kind of poem. Which is why I like the expansive kind of poem, because when I come home of an evening to sit down and do six or eight verses of it, what I've done or seen that day works its way in. That's what happened with the novel.

PJL: *Something like writing the kind of essay Montaigne wrote; it's a meditative method, isn't it?*

RA: Well, I think that basically I am an essayist. Certain of my strengths and many of my flaws point me in that direction. I think that one of my flaws is that too many things occur to me to say at once, and so I need a form in which I can accommodate that. If I tried to work in stricter forms I would simply bore the reader. There is no room in certain novels for three page disquisitions on something you just happened to have thought of, but there is in the kind of novel I ended up writing, and that I want to write again because I don't believe I did a really fine job in that first one. It was an experience. I still like it. It's fun to read.

PJL: *It is fun to read, especially to read aloud. I've heard your readings from excerpts and they are invariably effective with an audience. It begs to be read aloud, like Joyce.*

RA: I think all the rhetorical training I had in my early poems found its way into that book. It gave me a chance to play around with different voices and different levels of rhetoric. There's a lot of public speech of one kind or another in the novel, people lecturing, hectoring, recalling, arguing ....

PJL: *One thing that occurred to me the other night in rereading parts of* Hawryliw *is that it's in some ways an academic or anti-academic novel. Some of the voices, words and terminology sound familiar. It sounds like a graduate student blowing off steam, the result of years of listening to people orate, lecture about ideas, sometimes in a ridiculous fashion. You've been tuning in to the voices of the academy: you've also been tuning in to the voices of popular culture.*

RA: There are two things there, high and low culture meeting.

PJL: *Sandor Hawryliw and Oblong Cassidy .... Does writing a novel of ideas over such a long period of time require also other people to discuss your ideas with you? You obviously did an enormous amount of reading — your erudition has been commented on — but you also mention Stephen Luxton and Dave Brenner in your introductory note. You needed to talk to people?*

RA: In the early days of the novel Fred Turner did a lot for me. He too was writing a novel that was very eccentric and crazy, so we would work together and read each other sections of our work. That's possibly why it took the form it did and why the rhetoric is so obvious in it. Probably at one time or another I read everything aloud. I should mention Steve Luxton, who helped me tremendously with early drafts of the book. In one section I even got him to write a few pages to get me going again. Much of the tone and the form in *Hawryliw* I owe to the things Stephen and I did together in our early twenties, including a distant ancestor of *Hawryliw*, which we co-wrote. Dave Brenner, whom I mentioned earlier, worked out much of the mathematics and technical material of the book.

PJL: *The novel is not only digressive and lyrical but dialectical as well. You're contrasting opposing positions, sometimes starkly, then cutting across the opposition ironically.*

RA: Dialectical is a pretty fair term. In the end I conceived of it as a comic novel and a philosophical novel. The novel is set up so that there is one over-all narrator who includes all the other characters, all the other characters are part of him, or elements of his intellectual or emotional make-up. It's an almost medieval technique. Instead of dealing in abstracts you invent two characters who represent two separate things and you have them present an argument. It isn't done in quite that black and white a fashion, but each of the characters represents something, or a cluster of things, and more important-ly represents something to the other. What got me interested about half way through was the growing sense that we all love worlds of complete delusion that we placidly view as normality and try to impose on everyone else. So all the characters in the novel are victims of delusion, some misguided, some evil, some harmless, but they are all deluded. And just because they're deluded in eccentric and flamboyant ways doesn't change the fact that everyone lives like this, that people hold entirely irrational beliefs and structures of understanding about the world and no two people can agree on what the world is. Talk to a physicist and an artist and a farmer, and they'll all have entirely different senses of what the world is about.

PJL: *Have you discovered your own clue to the delusions? As you state it, it all sounds pretty bleak. We're all slightly mad.*

RA: Go back to *At Swim-of-Two-Birds*. That's a tremendously funny book, yet it's rather bleak too. It's a comedy ending in suicide.

PJL: *You, however, end with a reference to a butterfly.*

RA: Ah yes, the old story of the emperor and the butterfly. There's a lot of zen that worked its way into that novel. Whether it's the emperor dreaming he's a butterfly, or the butterfly dreaming he's the emperor, it was a reversal meant to suggest that, as in the world of sub-atomic physics, what you understand depends on where you are and how fast you're going. It's the same in the human world: you can't really say that things don't exist or that you can't understand them: it's simply that where you stand determines what you understand.

PJL: *In fact, there is nothing to resolve in this book. The dialectic is there, but neither of the antagonists Minden Sills or Sandor Hawryliw wins out or capitulates.*

RA: I can't reduce that novel to a single phrase. I think that the most important things are inexpressible, except that I don't operate in a world of metaphysics and religion so much. Most people locate the mysterious in a spiritual world. I don't. I try to locate it in the relationships between people and the understanding that people have between each other and the world.

PJL: *That certainly comes through in the poetry, in a compact and less intellectual form.*

RA: Yes, I agree. Although the novel is, remember, a product of my early to mid-twenties mostly so that a lot of the lumber of that novel is there simply because when you're at that age and are intoxicated with ideas they can all get in regardless. People have said that the first novel is the garbage can you've got to get out of the way before you start the second.

PJL: *What survives for you personally from that book?*

RA: Well, two things. One is the world of ideas and dialectics that I was dealing with. I think I have pretty firm notion of what I want to say and what I want to have my characters do. It's epistemological; that's my passion. It's what people know and how much they know it, how much they can count on the evidence of their own senses, how much they can know about other people's feelings and thoughts. The second aspect that is still with me after writing that book is technical. I think I know how to put together a long novel of a certain kind. There are certain kinds of books I would never try to write, but I think I can write a better *Hawryliw* that's more accessible, that's less encumbered with the baggage of the intellectual world but has at the same time more of the power of language and imagery.

PJL: Hawryliw *certainly shared attributes of some experimental fiction of the 70s. It's self-reflective, self-conscious, questions its own theory as it goes along and possesses fabulist and rhetorical elements.*

RA: Barth and Pynchon are both influences. They've both written good books that are going to be hard to improve on. I don't think *Gravity's Rainbow* is going to be improved on by Pynchon. Perhaps he'll surprise us, I don't know. And Barth's *The Sotweed Factor* is still one of my favourite books. He's come out with two or three other books in recent years, *Sabbatical* and *Letters*, and they're both incredibly ingenious and fantastically written. But you do get the sense that the ground has been gone over before and that it's become a trifle decadent.

PJL: *You remark in your* Moosehead *essay "Postmortemism," that much recent work of this kind has become self-indulgent and mannered. Yet* The Hawryliw Process *appears to be very much in the post-modernist mode. There appears a contradiction there.*

RA: Well, *Hawryliw* was a comedy and, despite the fact that I want the novel to be taken seriously, I tried not to take myself too seriously in the writing. I try not to have characters who speak ideas directly in a serious way; I would rather burlesque them and do cartoons of them and do slightly unrealistic and bizarre versions of things that are serious. In the end it's a comedy, a serious kind of comedy. A lot of post-modernist work takes itself in the dead serious sense of "we have finally found the key and now we're going to build a temple."

PJL: *One final question about* Hawryliw. *What about the book's reputation in Canada both at the time it was first published and in the years since? Some readers, notably the critic in* Books in Canada, *simply didn't comprehend what was going on: others more attuned to things that were happening else-where, were intrigued. Do you have any sense from talking to people, from listening to readers, of how the book has gone, how it has survived?*

RA: Most of the success it's had has been underground. I don't think reviews made a big difference in sales. It was published by a small press and the distribution wasn't great. There were twelve to fifteen reviews in the first year after publication of which about half were long and serious and received the book well. There were a couple which were dismissive and one or two reviewers were just out of their depth. I remember a review in *Quill & Quire* which was rather puzzled. Friendly but puzzled. I thought that when it was received quite well critically that this would be reflected in sales. It wasn't. It's sold quite slowly in the last six or seven years but whether there will be any place for it in the future I don't know.

PJL: *So after a year you left Prince Edward Island. There's a poem of yours which describes a train journey south from PEI to New York.*

RA: Yes, that was in my last book. I finally got a version of it that I liked after ten years.

PJL: *Let's use that poem to lead into our next line of inquiry. Frederick Turner remarks upon the image of the greyhound bus journeys which dom-inate your early poems. But much of your poetry, it seems to me, is "road"* *poetry. Travel seems to be an integral part of your imagination: you don't settle down for very long.*

RA: Well I like to travel myself and I can't separate that out from the characters in my novel or poems — because the poems have characters too. I think part of it is again epistomological and philosophical. This may sound mystical or silly or both, but in the sense I have of the world, when I close my eyes and try to see something essential about the world, it's like the theory of relativity. Things are in motion spacially and temporally. They can be known only in their relationship to one another and a relationship to a consciousness. A lot of the imagery in my poems begins with small things and ends up on a galactic scale with the movement of the stars, planets and galaxies back down to the small physical, intellectual and emotional movements of human beings. The image that springs to mind is almost medieval: the image of the spheres and everything in its appointed route, except of course that in modern nuclear physics it's all statistical and random and not predictable. Travel and movement bring with them the element of unpredictability. I think that's as close as I can get to what travel means in my poems.

PJL: *If you stopped travelling, you might stop writing poetry? Or would it be an entirely different kind of poetry?*

RA: I don't know. I think that my mind is so set in that way of looking at things now that I could probably stay in the same room for the rest of my life and write the same kind of thing. [pause] That's terrifying.

PJL: *This galactic sensibility is certainly in* Wintergarden.

RA: I was a big fan of science fiction when I was growing up and that influenced me too. Not only S.F. but various kinds of fantasy and fable, from picaresque novels and fairy tales to the travel literature of the ancients like *The Odyssey*, and the narratives of Roman geographers. I read them all the time. And nineteenth century writers like William Morris and Samuel Butler.

PJL: *It's curious that your own literary travel has been continental, south of the border to the United States and Mexico, east and west across Canada. You don't take those European and Caribbean trips people are so fond of. One of the rites of passage important to Canadian writers is the trip abroad. They've got to go somewhere else — far. But you don't.*

RA: It's almost as though subconsciously I've laid out the limits of my physical world and its the North American continent. I don't know why that should be. I think of Ammons who used to speak disparagingly of the rotten old stones of Venice and the decadent old world, which is an essentially American attitude. I feel bordered by the four oceans, but I feel at home here in North America even in some of the places I'd never lived, because they're too crazy or too intense or too violent or too empty. I feel North American, which is a silly thing to say because it sets you apart if you're a writer.

PJL: *Some nationalists would be suspicious of this continentalism.*

RA: Well, I'm not an economic continentalist. I'm not in favour of free trade or the Americanisation of Canada. Geographically I feel that way and only geographically. Canada has a very clear and distinct culture: it's different and ought to stay different. I'm still a nationalist in that sense. If there's going to be an economic union it ought to be on a world-wide basis.

PJL: *You cross the border easily.*

RA: I've lived very close to the border for twelve years so I physically cross it a lot. I see the differences.

PJL: *You've been in the Eastern Townships on and off since 1975 and you're back again after being in Montreal and on the west coast. What particular attraction do the Townships have for you?*

RA: I'm not a city dweller any more. I lived in Toronto in the 70s and it was good that I did because I was able to be part of what was happening there. But I think there comes a time when you need a bit of security and a little bit of isolation, time to dream, and think, and construct. I think that if there's any point in being a writer it's that you can spend a few years of your life making a record of what you lived and what you thought and what the world was like. After a while you don't need any more material for that. I like this kind of country: it's hilly, it's old, but it's settled and has a human element to it. It's connected historically with northern New England and with two important parts of the history of North America: the colonisation of the St. Lawrence Valley and the English colonisation of the thirteen colonies. One of my favourite books to this day is *Arundel* by Kenneth Roberts, which is the account of the American raid on Quebec city across the mountains of northern Maine. I feel as if I'm part of the history around here.

PJL: *The Townships, then, are a good place to write at least two of the kinds of poems that you write, those which relate to flora and fauna, landscape poems; and those which are satirical, sometimes grotesque, poems which comment on disasters on Tenerife and in the Andes. But there are others in which you are simply looking out the window in Ayer's Cliff.*

RA: That was something Michael Harris, who is editing the *Selected Poems*, pointed out: that many of the poems have a kind of framework provided by a window or a particular vantage point, that they begin with something almost like a painting. The two elements which you mention I can certainly recognise, but I don't see them as being exclusive or different. They seem to me to be part and parcel of the same thing. I've always felt that my work ought to reflect both the natural world and the world of human beings, that a lot of the argument about technological man trying to live in nature completely misses the point. It's all nature. It's nature that's been touched by us and changed by us, sometimes for the worse, but it's still all the same thing.

PJL: *So the old satirical dichotomy between city and country is, in your view, quite irrelevant.*

RA: Yes, I don't really think about that at all. I like to begin poems with a sense of the familiar and that usually means the natural world, but I'm always aware of the interpenetration of the natural world and the world of human beings, their ideas and technology. It's all the same. You can sit out in the country completely alone with your word processor and you're sitting at one of the nerve centres, writing as if the world is a brain, and we're all neurons. But another thing about the Townships is that it's reminiscent of England, which is where my earliest memories of landscape come from.

PJL: *You left England at what age?*

RA: Ten.

PJL: *So you have very distinct memories of the Bristol region?*

RA: And Somerset and Devon. It's not exactly the same sort of country, but there are enough similarities so that I can feel at home on some primeval level. Actually right now the landscape which is obsessing me is the desert. I was in New Mexico a couple of times in the last two years: it's absolutely wonderful: the sky, the light ....

PJL: *Could this be the source of another sequence of poems?*

RA: I don't know. I'm in a bit of a lull now and I'm not writing poems. I think it was the *Selected Poems* that did it for me. I spent an awful lot of time and energy putting together that book and in doing so I got some sort of perspective on what I had done over ten years. Now I want to work on another novel that I've been working on for two years called *Napoleon's Retreat*. It has Napoleon as a character but in three different incarnations: as the historical Napoleon, as a twelve-year-old boy living in the Toronto of the 1950s, and as that same boy later on in the 1980s working in an advertising agency.

PJL: *Anything can happen in a novel like that.*

RA: I don't quite know where it's going to go myself yet, which is probably why I was telling you all those things earlier about the novel having to grow. It's an apology for the fact that I'm pretty muddled about the shape of this book right now and I don't know what it's going to be, but I do know it's going to take a whole year of doing nothing else: I hope that'll be next year when I go on sabbatical. Other than that I've been writing a few short stories. But poems, no. I've come to the end of a chapter.

PJL: *That poem in* Wintergarden, *"Voyage to the Encantadas" breaks off unfinished. It describes a person recovering from the raptures of the deep and the consequent "bends" and he's back in "the valley of the Magog." Is the fact that the poem breaks off a symptom of what you have just described? Of having reached the end of a chapter?*

RA: Actually no, it isn't. I have that poem in draft; it's 150 pages long. That sort of poem takes a lot of work. I work on about four versions at any given time. The first version is 150 pages long. But even before I've finished that first draft I begin a second draft of about 75 pages. And before I get that far, I've begun a third draft which goes about 25 pages. And that's what you see in *Wintergarden*. That's all that was ready for publishing at the time. I've got plenty more but I don't dare to publish it until I'm sure of what it's going to be. You can't publish a poem in parts and then go back and say that part's coming out and change it completely. Once you commit it to print it's going to be there for a long time.

PJL: *Where did the idea come from?*

RA: There's another poem in the same book about Melville. Both poems came from the same time and the seed that was my reading of "The Encantadas" by Melville. I was reading a lot of Melville at the time, as well as a biography which described Melville living in a house in the Berkshires in Massachusetts in winter writing *Moby Dick*. I thought that was amazing; you get pretty severe winters in the Berkshires. It must have been like PEI or Quebec. There he was writing all this incredible, exotic stuff about sailing in the south seas looking for a great white whale, while living in the snowbound northeast. That became the idea of someone who lives here and voyages either in his head or recapitulates a real trip that he made over and over again in his head. It's an idea that goes back to the novel, the notion that with a very small amount of experience we can manufacture entire mental worlds for ourselves. So I conceived the idea of writing a long poem about this man recovering from a diving accident and coming home for the first time in ten years. He would give us the story of his life, not in a chronological way but going back and forth in various ways over his life, the kind of structure I picked up from Ammons and Stevens.

Technically there are two almost opposite things going on in that poem. One is that each line throws you for a loop further into a world that has to be somehow understood and yet at the same time each line and each word has to be right. It's the element I admire most in Stevens.

PJL: *Will it take another winter in PEI to complete the Napoleon novel?*

RA: [laughter] Another summer maybe. There was a time when I could write in all the little gaps of my life no matter how boring or crazy my life was. I think you become less and less capable of that. I've seen it in other writers; they become unstable and impossible to live with. It's a symptom of needing time and space. I think having a year off will solve a lot of problems that I've seen in my own writing in the past year. Not that I'm suffering from writer's block, but I haven't been able to give enough concentration to my work. We'll probably stay here. It's always nice to travel, but I know that if I end up travelling I'll end up writing less. For the past eight years or so I've been mining two or three different veins, and with the exception of "The Encantadas" I've finished all of them. I'm ready to to begin something entirely different. I hope this new novel will be that, but to do it I need freedom from the distractions of work, having to read theses, going to meetings, etc. It takes up enough of my mental and emotional energies that I find it difficult to write. I probably wouldn't be talking about this if I weren't steeling myself to write another novel. Part of the process of writing a long novel is fooling yourself into thinking you can do it, persuading yourself that you can actually run the 26 miles.

PJL: *So there's another marathon coming.*

RA: I hope so, because in the absence of a long novel to work on in the last seven or eight years I've become minimalist. That doesn't mean I haven't written things that are long, but I've concentrated on things that have very exact limits because that fits into the way I've been living and working. But I feel I want to throw down all those walls again and build something bigger.

Robert Allen was interviewed in Lennoxville, Québec, in 1987 by Philip Lanthier, then editor of Matrix. *It appeared in* Matrix #25.

Amitav Ghosh

Interviewed by **MERRILY WEISBORD**

MERRILY WEISBORD: *You're only 38, and you've produced an impressive body of work. Your academic training includes a B.A. in History, an M.A. in Sociology, a Diploma in Arabic and a D. Phil. in Social Anthropology. How did all this happen?*

AMITAV GHOSH: Since I was a boy, I always knew I would make my living by writing in some way. I never had any doubt about it. And I never tried anything else, really. I wanted to write and I wanted to travel. The two were indistinguishable.

After I finished my B.A., a friend and I wrote letters to about 60 countries offering our services as teachers. But if you're from India, or any Third World country, it's very hard to travel. For one thing, there's the question of money. And for another, nobody wants you because they think you're going to their country because you want to stay and make money. In fact, the only way you can travel, if you are a Third Worlder, is through academics.

When I was a student in India, I majored in History ... which meant I couldn't do anything else, because the way we are taught in India is incredibly specialized. But I became increasingly interested in looking at things from a different point of view, so I did an M.A. in Sociology, and then got a scholarship to Oxford. From there I went almost immediately to Egypt where I did the research for my D. Phil. in Anthropology. But finally I felt that the sorts of things I could say about Egypt, as an Indian and as an anthropologist, were so limited and so circumscribed that they were of no interest to me.

MW: *How did you collect the material for* In an Antique Land? *Was it the basis for your doctoral thesis?*

AG: The material for the parts in the village comes from my diaries. I have about 15 volumes of diaries.

MW: *You wrote these diaries when you were doing your field work?*

AG: Yes. And I had other material in my files. You know, doing field work was for me in many ways the beginning of my literary training. It sounds curious to say that, but I've never written as much as I did in that time. Every day I would sit down and write at least 3,000 words. I had files for what I thought of as hard facts, as I suppose most anthropologists do, and I'd fill those in first. And those are what made up my thesis in the end.

But of course, it was the diaries that were much more interesting, ultimately, than what went into the thesis. If you've ever kept a daily diary, you know what an exciting discipline it is. There just couldn't be a better discipline for a writer. Just trying to remember what people said, to remember their voices and how they said it, then to remember what the circumstances were, what the context was. Everything about the village in *In an Antique Land* is from a diary.

MW: *How did you develop the style we see in "Dancing in Cambodia" and* In an Antique Land? *You're creating a way of writing non-fiction that seems unique.*

AG: I'm trying to apply certain kinds of fictional techniques to non-fiction. That's common enough, I think. But one of the aspects of fictional technique that I'm trying to deal with, in particular, is temporal structures, and juxtaposing events in time and space.

MW: *Why is that?*

AG: I have always wanted to write simply. Not simple-mindedly, but in a way that would be lucid and available, to try to make a simple thing have many different kinds of meaning, just as some painters can compress a lot into a single line. And I've always been very concerned with time. Hemingway said that, for a writer, "Time is the enemy." There is always a fluidity to time within a novel. But I wanted to stretch that fluidity beyond "She thought of their last meeting ten years ago." I wanted to be able to make that eight centuries. So a novelist's way of writing allowed me to express many different kinds of ideas, to really enrich the writing of history.

I felt that history wasn't doing itself justice. History has become so academic, so boring really. But there is no reason why history should be written in boring ways. It's just that historians don't take narrative seriously. They think there are all these hard facts they have to set out, that arranging them is the soft stuff. But it isn't like that. The telling of history is something that belongs to the earliest expressions of mankind. It is the deepest kind of human need, a sort of self-location. And that need is only answered by narrative.

MW: *People say that you weave your stories. Do you like that description?*

AG: Do I think of it as weaving? No, that's not an image that comes to mind when I work. I prefer the image of the potter. I was struck by this when I was working on *In an Antique Land*, because when you write fiction the material comes into your mind already shaped in a certain way. But when you're dealing with non-fiction, you have the clay and you have to fashion it in certain ways and it offers you a kind of resistance simply because you're dealing with facts. To organize them elegantly, or to shape them into a narrative that will actually hold your attention, is very hard to do.

MW: *Why did you put yourself in the book?*

AG: There are many reasons why it's written in the first person. It's a point of view that I find easy to deal with, so it's useful to me in that sense. But, also, I wanted it there because I did not want to make claims for absolute objectivity. Because when you go to live in a village, or when you're travelling through Cambodia, a lot of things that happen around you happen because you are there. It's not truthful to pretend that it's all happening despite your presence and you're a fly on the wall watching it. You are, in a sense, at the centre of the narrative.

MW: *Yes. One of the parts I loved best is when you explain why you, an Indian who has seen so much religious violence, are terrified of symbols. Because in that part you're so clearly saying who you are, and what your intellectual baggage is.*

AG: And what my cultural baggage is, too. When dealing with a subject like that, I felt it very important to try to place myself within it, in a truthful kind of way.

MW: *Given your writing style, I wonder if you feel that the distinction between fiction and non-fiction is a valid one?*

AG: No. At the same time, it's not without its usefulness. After I finished *In an Antique Land*, Bill Buford, who runs Granta, said to me, "Well, what are we going to call this? Shall we put on a tag saying 'fiction'?" And I thought about it really hard and I said, "I wouldn't vouch for it that every word in this book is fact."

MW: *You recreated events.*

AG: But one thing I do know is that the book is not fiction. I didn't make it up. And I have 50 pages of footnotes. In a sense, that's the difference between fiction and non-fiction. When you're writing fiction, the act of imagining something already forms it. So it comes into your head at least partly formed. Whereas in non-fiction your material is outside you and doesn't come into your head fully formed. That clay is out there and its actuality is such that when you're trying to form it in certain ways, it resists you.

MW: *Did you want to leave that resistance behind — is that why you're writing a novel now?*

AG: I think of myself as a novelist. The other was much more of a diversion, really. I'll come back to it but in many ways it's very unrewarding to write a book like *In an Antique Land*, or even a piece like "Dancing in Cambodia," simply because they don't fall into the known categories. They puzzle people and they don't have the kind of saleability a novel might have. And it just takes so much work. You know, for *In an Antique Land*, I learned this whole new language [Judeo-Arabic, a language used in the Middle Ages], I learned this orthography.

MW: *How long did it take?*

AG: I'd been working on it on and off. By the time I wrote the book, I'd been working on aspects of it for 10 or 12 years. Just the very concentrated work took three years.

MW: *You have lived all over the world. Is this why the idea of dislocation is so important to you?*

AG: Yes. My life is lived in so many places — in Egypt, in India, in England and now, often, in America. My wife is in America, we spend half our time there. When I try and think about it, it really does seem to me often baffling. I mean, why have I ended up doing this, just being all over the place like this? But of course a lot of people do it; I think it's more common than not, for people to be all over the place.

You see, when you're outside your own country, living a life that is in some sense not a normal life, it's a very difficult thing to try to find a place for yourself within a global community. A space that allows you to say something which is not local, not read because it speaks for a minority, but has an appeal because it is universal, even though it speaks from the point of view of your own dislocation.

MW: *So your non-fiction is an attempt to deal with these personal concerns?*

AG: Oh, absolutely. I think that modern fiction, modern forms of literature and expression, simply don't give us images to think about this, which is our reality. Novels are still really constructed around a sense of place, a sense of rootedness. And really what I'm talking about here is a dissolution of location. I know that to be my reality.

MW: *Given this reality, where do you find your sense of community?*

AG: That's really often the hardest thing because that's what begins to seep away. One's community, in the end, becomes a community of choice. I have a very small group of very close friends who have been close friends since we first started college and are very literary people. We just grew up sharing books. And I guess I would say they are in some sense my community. But beyond that, it's family in both places, it's friends all around the world now, really.

MW: *Will you continue with creative non-fiction or will you write a third novel now?*

AG: What I writing now is definitely a novel. In an odd way it takes the style in which I've written non-fiction in a new and startling direction. I feel scared by this thing that I've been writing. You know, one of the things about dislocation is that it brings you in some curious way back to the notion of the supernatural. Because if you think of what a ghost is, a ghost is just a voice dislocated in space and time. This brings you back, by the oddest kind of hyper-modern root, to very old ideas about the supernatural.

MW: *What, in your background, has given you the moral stance that informs your work?*

AG: It's not that I write because I feel moralistically about the world. But I do feel strongly about things and that certainly does come into my work a lot. In some very general sense it must be because I grew up in Bengal, a highly political part of India, which was very strongly influenced by left-wing opinion. Even though I am not political in a straightforward way, I've absorbed things from my circumstances and my surroundings. And I have lived in Calcutta, which is a city where there is so much poverty and so much ... it's just in the air that there are certain things you have to think about and certain things you can't stop thinking about.

What I would say is that in my work, I try to look outside of myself, outside into the world, outside into things. Even when I'm writing in the first person, I don't think it is an introspective kind of writing. Really what interests me are other people.

MW: *You have said that when you look at the free market economy you find it bankrupt and heartless. Can you explain?*

AG: What the global media machinery tells us is that we've seen the end of ideology and that rational economics is going to triumph over everything. But that is not the case at all. In fact, when you create the kind of vacuum where there's no sort of good ideology to tell people how to live, the vacuum fills with trashy thinking — religious fundamentalism and ethnic fundamentalism of various kinds. I don't think it's a coincidence that we have seen the incredible rise of religious fundamentalism and ethnic ideologies going hand-in-hand with the triumph of the free market system. There is clearly some sort of correlation between the two.

MW: *What is that correlation?*

AG: It's hard to say. When you think back to 4 or 5 years ago, communism was collapsing and we were going to have a vast liberal world, in which everyone was vastly liberal and thinking about getting a new washing machine. It hasn't worked like that at all. It's been terribly violent. And one of the explanations we get is that we're in a period of transition. The other explanation is that these things were all bottled up under communism anyway. I just don't buy it. I don't think it works like that. I think what happens is that in any person, or in any society, there are many conflicting ideas. And the signals people get about what is permissible to think, what is good to think, in some sense condition what they think, or what they express.

If we begin to say that, for everyone, everywhere, the only thing that's worthwhile is just to get ahead, what happens to our notions of neighbourliness? Or notions of social duty? That you do have duties towards the people who live next to you? Unfortunately, I think what's really happened is that Western politicians and Western thinkers, in their eagerness to prey upon the end of the Cold War, to destroy Soviet domination, which was a horrible thing of course, propounded the idea that every nation should break away, everyone should be different, there should be this absolute right to self-determination, everywhere. But self-determination must go hand-in-hand with some notion of neighbourliness, some notion of collective living. Just because you put up a flag and say, "I'm a new nation," doesn't mean the nations around you are going to go away. There's got to be a point in time when we talk about the values and virtues of co-existence just as much as we talk about the values and virtues of increasing the GNP.

MW: *When you were interviewed publicly at the International Festival of Authors, the interviewer called* In an Antique Land *a pacifist book and you said you were looking for a voice with which to express non-violence. Was that a deliberate effort?*

AG: Very much so. Because *In an Antique Land* is about what must be the most incendiary subject that exists in our part of the world: the relationships between Jews and Arabs and the relationships between Hindus and Muslims. It is a subject so pregnant with the possibilities of violence that you have to approach it with a lot of respect and a lot of care. You asked about a moral stance: people like me come from a society where there is so much violence, so much religious violence, we have to think about the consequences of what we write. I wanted to write a book where difference wasn't necessarily the same thing as conflict. In a sense, that's what I learned in writing this book. That there have been points in time where people who consider themselves to have different beliefs do find modes of accommodating each other.

MW: *Do you still think that accommodation is possible?*

AG: Yes, I certainly do. I think if one didn't believe that, one would really be in a state of absolute despair. I think it's important to believe that, whether it's true or not.

Amitav Ghosh was interviewed by Montreal non-fiction writer Merrily Weisbord at the International Festival of Authors in Toronto. It appeared in Matrix #45.

Martin Amis

Interviewed by **BRENT BAMBURY**

BRENT BAMBURY: *Recently, in Britain, you were mistaken in* Time Out *for an exceptionally attractive young girl. Does this happen to you often?*

MARTIN AMIS: [laughing] Not any more. It stopped happening a long time ago. *Time Out* took a still from a film I was in when I was twelve or thirteen. But the still wasn't of me, it was of a young girl.

BB: *How were you cast in the first place?*

MA: Succession of accidents. My father knew the director, or my stepmother did. They were about to fly to Jamaica to start making a film but they hadn't cast the oldest boy. I looked right and sounded right. What they didn't bank on was that my voice dropped halfway through filming. And you know what they do then. An old lady dubs it! So you have this horribly hermaphroditic piping voice dubbed to what would have been me talking in falsetto.

BB: *Do you see the film now and again on television? Does it show up?*

MA: It's on every Christmas, just to haunt and shame me. [laughing]

BB: *Your kids have changed the way you live, the way you think, and I suppose the things that you write about. When* Einstein's Monsters *was published — a series of short stories that are direct and tangentially connected with nuclear threat — it seems like the press was taking you to task for the book. It was as if they thought you were too clever or too cynical to be writing something anti-nuclear. Were you surprised?*

MA: Well, I still get accused of adopting nuclear weapons as a career move. No one has actually said that I had children as a career move. The critics think it is a fashionable issue, which it isn't. It's not something people enjoy thinking about. It was more or less forced on me by having children and by suddenly seeing myself placed in time. People, like ourselves, born after the nuclear reality erected itself, don't have a terribly strong sense of time. We're the first people who've been asked in the history of the world to regard the world as expendable or mortal or likely to go bad. And I think that makes the future very contingent for us. But once you've got nippers, you've got to think in term of the future. It's just forced on you, willy-nilly.

BB: *You said it feels like you have a "best before" date stamped on you now.*

MA: That's right, "eat by ...." But that's more about turning forty and suddenly being on the front line of mortality with regard to your children. You know you're not going to survive them, they're going to survive you.

BB: *It's been said that* London Fields *is the first book of yours in which babies figure prominently as fictional characters. Was that a conscious choice?*

MA: They showed up in my conception of the book and I was delighted to see them. It really did feel like a new experience, writing in detail about children. I thought babies had never been outright comic figures or horror-comic figures. With one of the babies, Marmaduke, I think I did get to a new kind of comic character.

BB: *Yeah, he's the sort of hyper-maniac baby who isn't born in a delivery room but comes smashing through the window like a terrorist with a machine gun over his shoulder. A "cyber-baby!"*

MA: [laughing] Yeah, a "robo-baby!" I thought he worked very naturally as a comic creation. The other baby is a sweet little girl baby. I have two boys, needless to say. But the story works from a simple premise every parent knows — that each baby is both heaven and hell at the same time, in one package, usually with a nappie around it....

BB: *There are parts of London that you write about, that you seem so familiar with. I'm thinking of the pub on Portobello Road that's in* London Fields. *But I'm looking at you and you don't look like someone who could walk in unnoticed to a place like that. Did you have to research this book — get dirtied up and go down there and stand by the pinball machine? Or is this something that's all in your imagination?*

MA: Well, I said recently that low life, the type of life that I'm supposedly so immersed in, is really just something I drive through now in my German car!

BB: *Listening to music!*

MA: [laughing] Listening to music and sneering out the window .... Yeah, that pub did have a pinball machine in it. There's a lot I'll risk for a game of pinball .... But it's like all frightening places. it is six or seven times that you go in and then you realise you're not afraid anymore. Whatever murky un-understood life is within, suddenly you're accepted in it. Mind you, I wouldn't go in there in this Yves St. Laurent suit I'm wearing now.

BB: *Would you pull a shirt out of the dirty hamper and put it on?*

MA: Well, I wouldn't get that cultural about it. But I've spent my whole life being in places where I shouldn't really be. You get a feeling for what you can get away with.

BB: *Do you know the strategies of pinball?*

MA: Yeah, I'm pretty sophisticated. I have one in my kitchen.

BB: *What one?*

MA: *It's the one that's in the book — The Eye of the Tiger. It's a little battered now, but it's still got all the moves.*

BB: *How often do you play it? Do you use it as often as you use the food processor?*

MA: Oh, much more than that. I have to say that I work in a flat that is some distance from the house and, to my knowledge, not a meal has ever been cooked in this flat, but an awful lot of pinball gets played. I try to get down to about an hour-and-a-half a day.

BB: *This is a working machine ... I mean, when something isn't working out and you say "Damn!" — you get up and use the pinball machine and then go back and write some more?*

MA: That's right. Except that if you're trying to work something out while you're playing pinball, your pinball definitely suffers. There are tragic effects on your pinball. But you find after three quarters of an hour the difficulty that sent you to the pinball has evaporated and you're ready to go on.

BB: *There are three main characters in* London Fields, *four if you count the narrator, who needs to be counted. He's the voyeur. He's watching the other three characters and he's writing a book. At one point this narrator says something like, "Christ! What if people think I'm making this up!" I was wondering when you wrote that whether people say that to you, whether they actually say, "How does he do it?" "Why are his characters so grimy and so sleazy — with absolutely no principles at all?" Is this you watching you while you write this book?*

MA: Well, there is the distinction that while the narrator figure is an observer, as you say, a voyeur of this murder story that's taking shape around him, he wants to be anonymous. He suddenly imagines that people won't know that he's just being an observer and will assume that he has a very murky mind. People do look at me strangely when I enter a room sometimes. They don't want to be left alone with me. They don't realise that you really become another person when you enter your study, that certain demons descend on you there that have no part whatever your normal life. You may actually be polite and easy to get along with but you can become this giggling goo when you're writing. Comic invention, sinister intention, will take you to places that you wouldn't dream of going to in real life.

BB: *But the people who read your books and write about them equate those demons with you in some ways, don't they?*

MA: They do and that's why I have this, as you see, entirely unearned reputation for being difficult, nasty, insulting and all that. That's not for me, that's my work. People will come to see me and we will have a perfectly amiable hour together. But once they go home and they're in front of their word processors, they have to beat me up. It's the writer that makes them feel vulnerable and picked on, it's not me. It's the writer "me," not the civilian "me."

BB: *The writer of the book within the book* London Fields *is a Jewish-American writer named Sam. Sam is staying in London in the flat of Mark Asprey, the flat of a successful, pampered, media-adored person who shares your initials. Was that intentional?*

MA: Hmmm. In fact, there are lots of optional extras in this book. There are layers for some readers and and layers for others. But if you want to follow the Mark Asprey business through, then really he has cobbled the book together out of the remains left by Samson Young and published it pseudonymously under my name.

BB: *Mark Asprey seems like such a ridiculous character. He's perceived by others as almost a buffoon, a buffoon with special powers.*

MA: A sort of enviable buffoon. He's a successful writer but he represents all that his luggage would excite — envy without any real achievement. He's the sort of Barry Manilow of writing. Who was it who said that of Barry Manilow that everyone you know hates Barry Manilow's music but everyone you don't know thinks he's great? Mark Asprey is this concocted figure who is the popular writer, also taken seriously. The sort of devil that would haunt all writers, this worthlessly rewarded, talentless fraud.

BB: *Keith Talent, the first character our narrator is observing, is introduced as the baddest of the bad guys. But I think there is an admiration that you have for him. He's a cheat. He's easily flattered. He's a sort of cross between Bill Sykes and Malvolio. There are so many things in him that make you want to like him, even though he's truly a "bad" guy.*

MA: Well, he's the character, certainly in England, that everyone has praised the most, saying he will live in post-war fiction as the sleaziest possible creation yet. I did set out to test the reader's limits of sympathy. But the reader's sympathy always astounds writers by how capacious it is.

BB: *You didn't think that Keith Talent would be this popular?*

MA: No, I really didn't. I thought I was really taking a chance with him. Updike has speculated about this. He said there's no reason why we should like these vigorous villains. They're disgraceful creations. But the truth is that what we like is life, vigour, it doesn't matter which direction it goes in. A lot of people have taken Keith to their hearts. I've even talked to lady readers who said that they might even fancy him, if it weren't for the fact that he wore flared trousers.

BB: *That's a hard one to get over.*

MA: I think that is the real stumbling block in the end, the flares.

BB: *Tell me about darts, because Keith plays darts and darts are really his downfall. So you know as much about darts as you do about pinball?*

MA: Yes, I know a great deal about darts. I've felt that authentic darts gloom that comes over you after you've watched four or five hours of darts. I can't tell you how empty a man feels. One's character seems to be completely numbed and enervated by this crude form of human striving, which is what attracted me to it. It was the crudest form of human striving I could imagine ....

BB: London Fields *is set at the end of the millennium, but it takes a while before you realise the book is set in the future. Very little has changed over ten years except that the ecology seems to be self-destructing.*

MA: Well, all futuristic satire is really about the present. You're not making a sober attempt to imagine a future, although you put in a few details and you're also given a whole boatload of cheap jokes that you have to resist. But the end of the millennium is a real fascination of mine. I think it's going to be interesting, perhaps a bit too interesting. The end of the world is actually in the cards in a way that it never was before. You take elements like the worldwide resurgence of fundamentalism, the so-called 'plague' of AIDS, biblical distortions in global weather .... Nuclear weapons may seem like dinosaurs now with Gorbachev, but they're just as easily calibrating themselves as they were before. And the nineties will be the 'me' decade, the capital M, capital E. The Earth is not eternally young anymore. We all feel that. We feel the Earth is mortal. A huge ethic will be needed to preserve her. And what have we got in ten years time but a millennium. I'll be glad when we're past it. I really do think it's going to be a strange time.

BB: *You've lived in America and in England. Is London as horrible as some American cities have become?*

MA: Well, the narrator in *London Fields* speculates about this and quotes Saul Bellow's remark that anyone who is interested in the action on the leading edge of contemporary thought has to be in America because America is where the real modern action is. The narrator demurs and says that England is in the forefront of something, which is decay. We did everything first. We had our revolution early. We had our parliamentary democracy. We separated Church and state. We were out there. We got rid of our empire first. But now our big specialty is decline. The nature of that decline is rather different from the convulsions we see in American cities. It's not gunplay in the middle of the night and 'crack' wars. It's a more sullen form of degeneration. There's a definite feeling that there is a fixed gradient that we are sliding down. But the English nature is not one that objects to that kind of thing too much.

BB: *Or admits to it?*

MA: Well, I think they admit to it in what you would call the 'council flats' or 'projects'. Every now and then they have a riot about it. We have riots because the police are being asked to keep a lid on the underclass. Practically the first thing Margaret Thatcher did when she came into power was to cave in to a hugely inflationary police pay claim. She knew she'd be needing them along the line.

BB: *The character Mark Asprey in* London Fields *is afraid of London's poor. Are you?*

MA: I like to mingle, but not late at night. It's more distressing than frightening. You can't get very far down a London street that isn't in South Kensington or Mayfair without seeing some strange new profanity. In America, you can understand a mugging. That's a forced redistribution of wealth, under duress. But in England, it's more ragged, gratuitous, meaningless and often tied up with obscenity.

BB: *The narrator in* London Fields *says that America is a country going insane.*

MA: Huge forces are abroad in America that might take on terrifying shape at any minute. But what's happening in the cities — we all understand it — what's happening economically is that cities are changing into information centres and the last people to catch on to this are the ones who are still in the cities and forming the underclass there. And since America believes in arming its underclass, you have easily foreseeable results. England is a different story.

BB: *Your father, Kingsley Amis, is very funny when people talk to him about your writing. He always implies that he can't get through your books.*

MA: He doesn't imply it. He states it. We tend to snipe at each other in print, but when we meet we don't really go into it. Not that there's a frosty silence. It's just that we don't bother. People think that I must be very hurt by this. Maybe I was when it first happened, a long time ago, but he hates all modern writing. He's always saying that he can't bear these younger writers like Martin Amis and Julian Barnes and Ian MacEwen .... So I'm just in a list of people who he doesn't like. He even said, quite recently, that he will never again start a novel or continue with a novel that doesn't begin with the sentence — "A shot rang out."

BB: *[laughing] You have a good relationship with him.*

MA: Yeah, very good.

BB: *Did you ever say to him, "I'm going to be a writer."*

MA: What he never said to me was. "Go ahead, become a writer." It was probably natural indolence on his part. He never encouraged me, but I know quite a few writers who encourage their children to write and it almost always spells the end of the relationship. Writing talent doesn't seem to be very strongly inherited. For a writer to say to his son "go with these poems, they're very good, you're a genius" is almost like the son saying to the father "you can be me, you can have my life." A very complicated, very murky offer. The son may go on thinking for a little bit that he is a genius. But it won't work out. I think my father and I are one of the few cases of it working out, where we both have a corpus of work.

BB: *Are you eager to write something short now after* London Fields*?*

MA: Yes, something very short and something light. Although I'm writing a short story at the moment which has to do, glancingly, with the Jewish holocaust. So, as you can imagine, I'm feeling incredibly wary, wondering what George Steiner will think and so on.

BB: *Why did you make the narrator of* London Fields *Jewish?*

MA: It's a literary idea, really. The Jewishness is significant for the internal reason that the Jewish Holocaust is the only event that prepares our imaginations for a nuclear holocaust. It was so the character would have some understanding in his heart and his soul about the enormity of that.

BB: *You recently returned from Houston where you were on the set of* Robo Cop II*. How did that happen?*

MA: The editor of *Premiere* magazine. He realised that it had to be an interesting assignment to get me out of the house. He knew I adored Robo Cop, so he had me with Robo Cop II.

BB: *Your taste in films runs towards the cyberpunk?*

MA: Well, *Blade Runner* is another one of my favourite films. The cinema is just becoming capable of doing what science fiction writers have been doing since the thirties — imagining a real future. And that increasingly seems to be what novelists of my age are doing. We're jumping a little way into the future. Perhaps one of the reasons for this is that the future isn't guaranteed anymore, so we'd like to visit it now, while we still can.

Broadcaster Brent Bambury spoke to Martin Amis on CBC Radio's Brave New Waves, shortly after the publication of London Fields. *The transcribed interview appeared a year later in* Matrix #33.

Neil Bissoondath

Interviewed by **P. Scott Lawrence**

P. Scott Lawrence: *What made you decide to break from the fiction writer's cover and plunge into this perilous debate? [The debate about multiculturalism that arose after the publication of* Selling Illusions *in 1990]*

Neil Bissoondath: I suppose what you're really asking is why I've written a non-fiction book of a somewhat pugnacious kind. I've been thinking and writing about multiculturalism for a long time. In recent years, the Reform Party has been making its own criticism of multiculturalism, and a lot of that criticism has been cast in racial terms. Those are terms that make me uneasy. So I feel that we have long needed to have a debate, and I didn't like the Reform's take on it.

So, *Selling Illusions* is really a book aimed at helping a real discussion get going. I hope it will allow people who have also had hesitations about multiculturalism to find the desire, or the courage, to start speaking out about their real feelings.

PSL: *In the book's subtitle, you refer to multiculturalism as a cult. Why?*

NB: Oh, that's very simple. Multiculturalism is enshrined in government legislation, and like all public policy, it should be open to criticism, to evaluation. But for twenty years there have been fairly successful attempts to protect multiculturalism from real scrutiny. I've been called an Uncle Tom, a sellout, a racist, for my views. A multicultural bureaucrat in Ottawa once told me to shut up with my criticism, because I was encouraging racists like the Reform Party. So the attitude has been that the rules are established, and you break them at your own peril. That is exactly how a cult operates.

PSL: *What's at the heart of your quarrel with multiculturalism?*

NB: I think there are three bases, really. First of all, multiculturalism fails to fulfill its stated purpose of preserving an individual's culture. There are a number of reasons for that. The very act of immigration changes you, in the first place. When you get on a plane, not as a tourist, but as someone going to a new land forever, you become a very different person. And you don't come here looking, expecting, or wanting to preserve the culture you've left behind. That is not your concern. So the act asks of immigrants and new Canadians something that is alien to them.

PSL: *One presumes you've left your homeland for a reason.*

NB: You've left for a reason, exactly, and you're not coming here to play ethnic.

PSL: *And the policy encourages that?*

NB: The policy, of course, encourages that. So, it's untrue to the individual. On the second level, we've got the idea of promoting these various cultures. But you cannot promote something as complex as a culture. So, we have simplified the notion, we have taken it and we have turned it into something we can package and put on a stage. But the real depth of a culture, the beauty and the ugliness, the thousands of years of art and history and philosophy, none of that has any place in our concept of multiculturalism. We are quite happy with Disneyland. It's theatre, it's trivialization.

PSL: *But it seems to me that this Disneyland can only exist if there are willing participants in the spectacle, if there are performers.*

NB: Yes absolutely, but people are told that this is the correct thing to do, that this is what one must do. And that gets me to the third point, the third level of betrayal of this policy, and I'm talking here not so much politically as psychologically. The policy tells newcomers, new Canadians, that what they find here is less important than what they have left behind. The message is sent out that you must live apart from this society, never fully engaging with it. Yes, you go out and you get your job, but then you go home and you make sure that, at home, within your ethnic community, you work at preserving the past. This is your role in creating this so-called mosaic. The policy tells them that this society doesn't really matter.

PSL: *Do you see these issues as fitting in with the concerns of your fiction in any way? Or is your subject matter here utterly different?*

NB: The whole issue of multiculturalism and the way we've approached it deals with a sense of belonging, and now how much one feels one belongs to this country and how much you're allowed to belong. Those are questions that, I think, inform my fiction. A lot of my fiction grows out of fears of not belonging, fears of not being accepted, things that I don't feel personally, but which are there nevertheless.

PSL: *You do feel a sense of belonging in Canada, then?*

NB: Very much so.

PSL: *Why is that, do you think?*

NB: Time; luck perhaps. I have lived here more than half my life, and I left a country to which I never felt I belonged. Very quickly, after coming to Canada, I found myself making friends and fitting in, which, of course, was a kind of a surprise. Over the more than two decades that I've been here I've travelled a great deal and I've found myself to be comfortable wherever I've gone. Of course, a lot of that has to do with the reception I've received from other people. But out of those experiences grew of itself a sense that this place had become home. Which was a new concept for me, the idea of home.

PSL: *What was it that never allowed you to feel a sense of belonging in Trinidad, a sense of home?*

NB: It's very difficult to explain. There was an attempt, early on, to inculcate me into the new Trinidad, the independent Trinidad, but maybe it was my cynicism, maybe it was my dissatisfaction at not getting the books and the movies that I was reading about but just weren't available. Or the sense of being on the edge of things. The sense that there were too many hypocrisies around me, too much racism within my family and in the surrounding society, a society divided along racial lines. So, I grew up with this feeling of not belonging to this place, of knowing that one day I would leave it.

PSL: *Those who defend multicultural policy argue that it is necessary because Canadian society is systematically racist, and this has prevented them from feeling that they belonged.*

NB: I've been incredibly lucky; I have not had any racist experiences. I have dealt with honourable people. None of which prevents me from saying that there is racism in this society; I know there is, I'm not that naive. At the same time, the charge of systematic racism is a blanket generalization, levelled against what is seen as a white society, particularly a white male society. If I were to say something such as, gee, blacks are lazy, or Chinese can't drive because of the shape of their eyes, or Indians are drunks, that would be an equally blanket generalization. That's what I think the charge of systematic racism is; a blanket accusation that is very easily used to manipulate the good will in this society. So, I simply don't buy it.

PSL: *If there is good will in this society, and if it is easily manipulated, why do you think that's so?*

NB: There is nothing quite like good old white liberal guilt. It leads sincere men and women to act something like the old colonized people who would try really hard to be like the colonial master — the Indian who turns himself into the perfect Englishman, for instance. What we have today are white liberals who go out of their way to be more ethnic than the ethnics, more coloured than people of colour. And that often comes from, or so it seems to me, a lack of historical perspective, and a historical kind of guilt that is easily subject to manipulation.

PSL: *You've been here for over 20 years now. Do you still run into people who ask you what your nationality is?*

NB: All the time. And when you are mischievious enough to reply, "Canadian," immediately comes the response: "Yes, but what nationality are you really?" Look at the implications of this. First of all, it would seem not sufficient to be simply a Canadian. Second, you're being viewed as an exotic creature. And so long as people see you as the other, as not being fully part of the landscape, you will always be marginalized. That goes not only for you, who may have come from another country, but for your children, too.

PSL: *In a certain way, too, to hyphenate you also permits me never to have to consider the country as truly and fundamentally multi-racial.*

NB: Exactly. It is a policy that allows the best-intentioned people, still, to have a vision of division. It allows people to view Ben Johnson as the Canadian who won Olympic gold, and the Jamaican immigrant who lost it.

PSL: *You mentioned earlier that you'd been castigated for your views. In fact, there have been some fairly harsh attacks. One critic has charged that you "pimp the tawdry racist views of colonial powers, past and present, the* *world over." This same writer claimed that "authors like V.S. Naipaul and his nephew, Neil Bissoondath, are both examples of writers who catapulted to fame on the savage and, at times, racist critique of the Third World."*

NB: Marlene Nourbese Philip made these remarks in a couple of essays. These are, of course, the kinds of political accusations that are brought to my fiction by people who disagree with me politically. She criticised me also for presenting Fidel Castro in a negative light. I have to say that I do have a political stance, as does she. I do not believe that I — or V.S. Naipaul — have ever apologized for colonialism. We may not have taken what on the left would be seen as the politically correct stand, but I have no apologies to make for that. I am not an idealogue, and idealogues of the left will certainly make these kinds of accusations. I can't say it bothers me. It is so overstated as to be absurd.

PSL: You've also been accused of "shitting on the country of your birth."

NB: Yes, well, people have, from the beginning, expected me to be a propagandist for the Caribbean. I have never seen my role as a fiction writer as one of propagandist. I haven't "shitted on the country of my birth;" I have tried when I've written about Trinidad, or the Caribbean, to capture some of the realities that the tourist industry would rather not have known. If writing as honestly as one can about both the sunshine and the shadows means that I'm shitting on the country of my birth, so be it.

PSL: *So what does it take for you to lose your remarkably even temper?*

NB: It takes a great deal, because this kind of language is so stereotypical, and the vision is such a clichéd one, that it's hard to really take it seriously. The only thing that really stings me is when I get a review for a novel that I feel isn't fair. I'm not talking about the negative review — negative reviews are fine, and often if a negative review is intelligently written I will learn something. But there have been a couple of occasions when I have received what were patently unfair reviews, reviews which had me suspecting that the person hadn't read my book, or had imposed an ideological vision so stringently on what I had written, that they hadn't seen what I had written. That bothers me, and at times like that I tend to indulge in fantasies of violence, and then eventually let it go. That's part of the game.

PSL: *But it does seem these days that ideologically severe positions enjoy a certain currency in Canadian artistic circles.*

NB: I wonder how much sway these views hold in the public at large. Take the whole argument over the appropriation of voice. I have the impression, from students and the public that I've been running into, that people can't believe that we take this crap seriously.

PSL: *But an argument might be: Look, I have been silenced historically, and I'm tired of having people whom I identify as my oppressors speaking through me or for me.*

NB: No one is preventing these people from speaking for themselves. And preventing others from writing through the voice of a native character or a black character does nothing to create a space for your own voice. It is simple censorship, and it is absurd to claim that demanding silence of others somehow gives you a forum. You have a forum anyway, but the forum is being used to make political complaints, the forum is being used to shed tears, and it's being used to manipulate emotionally and politically, instead of being used for the presentation of your art.

PSL: *But it is the view of some that there is racism in the publishing industry, and that's why these voices aren't being heard.*

NB: If I may be blunt, I think the notion is absurd. I'm not saying there is no racism in publishing, there is racism everywhere. But the complaint that one has not been published because of systematic racism strikes me more often than not as simply an excuse for failure. People who don't write very well or who don't write enough, and who complain that the work that they do should be published simply because they are of a particular ethnic background — it's an excuse. It's another example of this cultural victimization: poor me, I'm always being done in.

I think we can take a look at the kinds of people who have been published in this country in recent years, we can take a look at the enthusiasm with which Canadian publishers are searching out good writing of all kinds, and say that this is nonsense, that the people who make these complaints are looking for a kind of artistic welfare, nothing more.

PSL: *Nevertheless, these issues do raise questions of who artists can speak for and through, and questions about their social function.*

NB: Writers have no social function. Writers have one function, and that is to tell a good story. What you want to do with the telling of that good story is very personal. I know that what takes me through the writing of a novel is simply the desire to understand imaginary lives very different from my own.

PSL: *Is that your prime motivation?*

NB: Yes. And if people read my books and are entertained by them, and maybe learn something about those lives, I'm very satisfied. I'm not a cultural worker of any kind, I'm not here to build some kind of cultural edifice for this land. Real art cannot proceed from that kind of instigation. It comes from a much deeper and much more emotional grounding.

PSL: *Behind all these concerns, though, is a genuine desire to address social imbalances.*

NB: These imbalances have to be addressed with time. The Ontario government has just passed into law its unemployment equity legislation. It talks about having the Ontario civil service reflect the ethnic makeup of Ontario. Which means that they have to have percentages. Such a percentage of the Ontario civil service must be black people, such a percentage Chinese. I'm not sure how far they're going to go, but let us hope that they one day won't decide that they will measure how many bisexual mulattos they must have, because that's the kind of thinking that we're engaging. I know it sounds absurd, but we are dealing here with a government that is measuring ethnicity. And that makes me uneasy, because a racial vision easily turns into a racist vision.

PSL: *But what's the alternative?*

NB: As an individual, as a human being, I would much rather have a system that from the beginning makes an attempt to be colour-blind. I want to see a hiring practice that isn't so concerned with how the civil service looks, but how it performs. So that when we start looking for people, we don't ask them what colour they are; we ask them instead what their qualifications are.

Now, let's say we have parity between two people. One person happens to be pink, one person happens to be brown. So we decide at that point, okay, in the name of a certain equity we can make a discriminatory choice here and hire the brown person. But when you from the very beginning practice racial discrimination, when you have ads in the newspaper eliminating people who are white, you are setting off on the wrong track.

PSL: *The problem with that approach is that change might be glacial.*

NB: I don't believe in revolution. Revolution anywhere has led to chaos. I do believe that the best approach is one that does not discriminate, that will attempt to give equal opportunity to everyone in this society, including white males. It may be slow, glacial maybe, but eventually, if we do not discriminate, these people will catch up. It's part of the lesson of Canadian history. The Italians, or the Jews, or the Irish, or the Japanese, arrived at one point, suffered through a period of discrimination, sometimes very serious discrimination, and then — through effort, through work, through education — made their way into the mainstream. They are now fully part of Canadian society. That's the kind of thing that I think we need to do, rather than these artificial programs that could lead to incompetence and will lead to resentment.

PSL: *Let me play devil's advocate for a moment. Neil Bissoondath, how dare you, as a privileged member of our cultural elite, attack our multiculturalist ways, and come down on the side of elitist policies? By your own account you have not suffered the kind of racism that so many people have. So how can you understand the problems of the marginalized, given the situation you're in?*

NB: I wasn't born into this situation. I made my way into this situation. I worked my way into this situation. I didn't approach publishers with the demand that they had to publish my first book because I was a brown-skinned male. Neither did I approach publishers saying you must publish my book because I am the nephew of V.S. Naipaul. I did my work, I wrote my book, I worked very hard at it. When I was writing my first book I was living from hand to mouth as a teacher. I was barely paying my bills; at times I wasn't. But I wasn't about to use that, or the colour of my skin as an excuse. What I am saying is that too many people use these things as excuses. We have legitimized the idea of victimization in this society, the idea that you are hard done by.

PSL: *How do we instill the values of this society in newcomers without trampling on their beliefs? When is it all right for one man to wear a turban?*

NB: Part of what I'm saying in this book is that we have to decide as Canadians where these lines must be drawn. We have to stop saying to new Canadians that your ancestral homeland is more important than here. What we have to start saying is that, yes, your past, your parents' past, your grandparents' past, all these that have come together to create you and bring you to this land are vital. You must know your place in the world. But you must also recognize that that ancestral land belonged to your parents and your grandparents — it does not belong to you. They came here to give you a different chance, a new country; it is up to you to take advantage of it.

PSL: *But — to cite an example you use in the book — if it's part of my belief system that I should be able to insist that my daughter be circumcised, yet the practice contravenes Canadian mores, what do we do?*

NB: One of the things we have not done, particularly in English Canada, is establish those boundaries. When you come here there are no clear rules to follow. There is a basic rule of law, but there are no ideas to which you must dedicate yourself. And what we have to do is decide that, yes, there are values and ideas that we believe in as Canadians, and make it clear to newcomers that there are things that are simply not acceptable. Yes, in your society and your culture, infibulation may indeed be vital ... but in our culture, we have decided that no, this is mutilation, this is not acceptable. That discussion has evaded us because we're not sure who the hell we are, or what we believe in. And we're also afraid to offend.

Multiculturalism tells us that by trying to put limits on the cultural expression of the various groups coming here we are being offensive to them, we are being imperialist. We have to start realizing that this is not so, that we too have values. That we must have values.

PSL: *As we both know, Québec is a distinct society. Has it managed things differently from the rest of Canada?*

NB: I think it has, and in one very important way. While English Canada has drifted in a chaos of values, Québec has not. English Canada lost the old colonial British sense of itself, and has replaced it with nothing. Québec has remade itself in the last decades, but it's become a modern vibrant society without ever losing its sense of itself. As a newcomer to this country, if you go to English Canada, everything is up for grabs. You have a clearer idea of where you stand in Québec. You have a sense of just how far you can go. And the surrounding society has a sense — which is the beginning of dialogue — of just how far it is willing to let others go.

PSL: *But the question of who is a real Québécois has always been a troubling one here.*

NB: But I think that people have been rethinking this whole question. The old answer, the racial answer, is, I believe, increasingly unacceptable to the younger generation of Québec nationalists. There's a lot of evidence for that.

PSL: *Even so, one hears all the time of* Québécois pure laine *referred to as a 'people'. This is a strictly ethnic definition. And it comes not just from the fringes of the nationalist movement, but from the leaders of the Parti Québécois.*

NB: But the Parti Québécois is in so many ways the party of the old nationalists. Their thinking is on the way out, I believe, and they know it. This is an impression, but it's a heartening impression. And, as a member of several minorities, I feel good about the fact that there are at least people out there thinking, posing the hard questions, people like Lise Bissonnette [publisher of *Le Devoir*, a prominent Québec daily] who calls the whole idea of a *Québécois de souche* or a *Québécois pure laine* racist, and other editorials talking about breaking away from the old Québec parochialism.

PSL: *You now belong to a sort of exemplary end-of-20th-century family. As you point out in the book, you might be seen as Indian-Trinidadian-West-Indian; your companion is Franco-Québécoise-Canadian; and the list of hyphens your daughter can lay claim to is staggering. How does this influence the way you feel about these things?*

NB: I suppose that it influences the fact that I wrote the book. And it has sharpened my sense of urgency about the debate. My daughter Elyssa will grow up a bilingual girl with dark skin, black hair and dark eyes. And she will have to fit into the society. If we continue constructing a society based on a racial vision of the population, she will be worse off for it. If we move instead towards a society that considers all of us to be simply Canadians, of different backgrounds, and we leave those backgrounds to inform those individuals, to give those individuals strength, then I think she'll be better off for it.

P. Scott Lawrence, a published writer of fiction himself, interviewed Neil Bissoondath in NDG, Montreal, where he then lived. The interview appeared in Matrix *#44.*

Michael Crummey

Interviewed by **LYNN DONAGHUE** and
VICTOR COLEMAN

MICHAEL CRUMMEY: My father fished until he was seventeen; he started when he was nine. It wasn't unusual for young boys to fish, but that was a bit young, even for Newfoundland. My grandmother was afraid that Dad was going to kill himself. She felt that she didn't have a lot of control over him. She thought he'd be safer down on the Labrador Coast with his father. There were ten to fifteen thousand Newfoundlanders who left the island in the early spring for the coast of Labrador, either as stationaries, where they owned a piece of land, or as floaters, on boats, where they'd spend the whole time. Dad would have to leave school early and start late in the fall. They usually arrived late in May or early June. According to how fishing went, they'd be down there until mid to late September, sometimes as late as October.

Dad's father died when he was sixteen. Basically [my grandfather] would hire a fishing crew every year, three or four men who would go down with him, and he would pay them at the end of the season based on their catch. My dad had to take over when my grandfather died; but the fishery had pretty much gone by then, at least in that area.

I can remember, when I was a kid, seeing stuff in the papers about the inshore fishermen saying that the cod stocks were going down and if they didn't do something they'd lose them altogether. So after two seasons [my dad] was $200 in debt, which in '46 or '47 was a lot of money. So he got the [mining] job in Buchans, to pay off the debt. But then they never left. In Buchans they had heated buildings and flush toilets and a regular paycheque. The fishing was brutal work; I think they found working at the mine pretty easy — he thought he was living the high life — but he never actually went underground. He had to lie about his age to get the job in the first place. He was only sixteen and you had to be nineteen to go underground, which paid more money, so he said he was eighteen and then never went underground, which was probably a good thing. I'm glad he never did.

In Buchans they were mining a little bit of everything. It was primarily a zinc mine; but there was lead, copper, silver, gold. And it was a 'company store' kind of arrangement. The only way into town was by company train, and if they decided they didn't want you in there they'd put you back on the company train and you were gone. There was no way to get back in. Everything in the town was owned by the company, the store was owned by the company, the theatre was owned by the company, the bowling alley was owned by the company, the rink was owned by the company. In Buchans, it was the American Smelting and Mining Company; I think that was the only place in Newfoundland they operated. It wasn't the same sort of monopoly that you see in Nova Scotia and New Brunswick with Irving where they own every fucking thing in the province.

It was a weird situation because the actual rights to the Buchans property were owned by Price Abitibi, so ASMACO actually had to pay some unbelievable amount of their profits to Price-Abitibi. And they used that as an excuse to pay really bad wages. When my dad got laid off from the Buchans he'd been there for thirty years — this was 1979 — I think he was making $12,000 a year, and he got a job about a year later in Wabush, Labrador. When he applied there he was too embarrassed to put down how much he'd been making. When he started in Wabush he was making about three times what he made at Buchans.

My stories [as collected in *Flesh and Blood*, Beach Holme, 1998] deal more with Buchans. A lot of the stories are set there but they don't really have much to do with the town. When I was writing *Hard Light* [Brick Books, 1998] a big part of what I was hoping to do was to give a sense of what life was like in that community. In some of the stories that was the case as well — what it was like to live in a mining town. But in other stories it was just about this family and the town really had nothing to do with it. I don't know if that gives [the collection] a bit of an uneven quality or not. I still feel I'm a bit lost with stories.

I started writing, really writing, six or seven years ago. I'm still not really comfortable with writing fiction — the story form, what makes a story work — I'm not sure of the difference between a story that works for someone and one that doesn't. With poetry — or even with short narrative pieces — I had a pretty good idea about when something worked or didn't, what I could do to try and fix it if I thought it wasn't working. With the stories I felt totally lost. I had no clue. When *Flesh and Blood* was first accepted for publication I was a bit freaked out actually. But the editing process was really helpful — very painful — whereas the editing process for *Hard Light* was a lot of fun. That's partly because I thought it was a good book when it started. And the guy who was editing it [Gary Draper] loved it. It was a really enjoyable experience. We sent the manuscript back and forth five or six times, we spoke on the phone four or five times, and then I went to see him. And he had no real background in the content of the book. I felt quite comfortable disagreeing with [some of

Gary's editorial suggestions]. I felt like we were having a conversation.

The editing for the stories was much more painful, because it needed a lot more work. All of the stories in the book are one to four pages shorter than they were when we started. When I first got the manuscript back from Joy Gugeler [the publisher] I was pretty upset, until I sat down and actually looked at the suggestions that were being made. I think I made about eighty percent of the changes that she suggested, which was mainly cutting out and moving stuff around so it fit together better. On a few occasions, I thought she hadn't gone far enough and I ended up going further. The stories are much better as a result. They're cleaner. I think I was explaining too much.

I've never been very good at being elliptical. It was good to have someone go through it and say you don't need this and you don't need that.

LYNN DONAGHUE: *What brought you to Kingston?*

MC: School. Graduate work. It was awful, I hated it. I've been there now, let's see, eleven years. I did a one-year Masters, which was horrible, and I thought, well, maybe I just had a bad year. I really had no clue about what I wanted to do with my life. Halfway through the first year of a PhD I knew I was quitting, but I had a scholarship that I'd have to pay back if I didn't finish, so I finished the year. Everyone I talked to hated the [Queens U.] English Department. But also I was just a terrible grad student. I was a really good undergraduate. I knew how to give profs what they wanted; and I thought about my work, which is more than a lot of others did. I didn't take [graduate studies] seriously enough to want to put that much time into it. And I don't think I was "smart" enough, in that way. I didn't get literary theory. Stuff that now seems pretty straightforward made no sense to me at all in my fifth year as an undergraduate. Simple things like the basic tenets of deconstruction — I had no idea. So I don't think I was ready for grad school.

Part of the reason I took an English degree was it was the only way I knew of to be legitimately connected to the whole idea of writing, literature, without actually admitting to anybody that I wanted to be a writer. I was in the closet, big time. I didn't tell a soul. Not one person. Although from the age of sixteen, probably, I was writing every day. I was too shy. I thought [my writing] sucked, which was a combination of insecurity and the fact that I actually did [suck].

I remember having a big fat anthology of British, American and Canadian poetry, which was what introduced me to poetry. And I thought: This is amazing stuff, and I want to do it. It was all 20th century stuff that I read — other stuff really didn't do much for me — I mean, Leonard Cohen was a big one. I was sixteen. William Carlos Williams, Frank O'Hara — I was really into Sylvia Plath when I first started reading poetry. Comparing anything I was writing to one of those people was a really painful process. That's why I was incapable of talking about it. The other thing was that the only other people I'd ever met who said they wanted to be writers seemed unbelievably pompous to me. I didn't want anyone to look at me like that. And, also, I didn't know that many people in Kingston. I was pathologically shy up until the age of 24 or 25, painfully shy. I was the kind of kid in Newfoundland that, if my mom sent me to the store to get something, and I couldn't find it on the shelf, I couldn't go to somebody ....

VICTOR COLEMAN: *I noticed that in* Hard Light; *you're not there most of the time.*

MC: Yeah. I'm sort of like the book-ends to the book. The only time I speak of myself is in the third person. There's a lot more of me in the first book [*Arguments with Gravity*, Quarry Press, 1996]. In *Hard Light* it would have felt fake to put more of me in there. Part of the point for me when I came back to work on it is that I am absent from that, that I've always been absent from that. When I was growing up in the mining town I was totally separate from everything that most people think of when they think of Newfoundland, like my father, who grew up with it — from the age of nine he was fishing. So that split was always really obvious to me. Because of that I've always been obsessed with my father's life.

VC: *Whereas he was probably thinking, at the time: There's no way a son of mine is going to go out fishing when he's nine years old.*

MC: Dad quit school when he was sixteen, after his father died. My uncle, who's a teacher, always said that my dad had more brains in his little finger than the rest of the family combined. He's a very intelligent man. He didn't like school, he grew up working, and that's what he knew. When it came to his children, school was it. I think we were lucky. I never felt any intense pressure to live up to something I could never live up to.

I'm the second oldest of four boys; but I was always treated as the youngest, partly because I cultivated that, and partly because I was the only one who really had no clue what I was doing with my life. Part of that was knowing, in the back of my mind, that I wanted to write. But I never felt that I could say that, it wasn't an option. Compared to my brothers, I read a fair bit when I was growing up; but we all knew the alphabet before we went to school. My mom would cut out the letters and put them on the fridge. And she read to us. I was probably more interested in reading than the others. I really loved it. Although I've never been what you would call a voracious reader. I'm pretty slow, for one thing, which makes it difficult. When I was ten, eleven, twelve, I was reading some awful piece of American propaganda dressed up as a kid's novel; and I remember some cowboy book. I wasn't reading Dickens when I was twelve. I was a slow developer. I wouldn't have gotten Dickens. It wasn't until that first year of university — which I actually did in my home town in Labrador when you could do that — when I got that anthology, that something clicked. And I was hooked and I decided that I wanted to do something with this. I remember going to the back of the library to one of those little carrels and hiding away at the back there and deciding that I was going to sit down and write a poem. I might have written three or four rhyming things in high school, but that was it. I'd made the decision: I was going to try and write poetry. And I never stopped. I started writing then and I wrote constantly and have pretty much since. Partly one of my big weaknesses as a writer is that I'm poorly read. In university I focused almost exclusively on Canadian literature, and that's a weakness. In the last three or four years I've been reading more literature that isn't Canadian, just to get a sense of what's out there. But I don't feel impoverished because of that.

As an undergraduate at Memorial [University of Newfoundland] I had to do a full course in the history of the English language, and another in Old English, which was good; but not a single American course. So I guess I'm trying to fill some holes. I'm just starting to find writers now that I'm interested in.

VC: *You won a literary award at Memorial. What did it do for you?*

MC: I had seen a notice for the award posted somewhere, and I'd been writing for about four years and hadn't shown anything to anyone. I may have quit a couple of times the previous year, thinking this is just crap, I'll never amount to anything as a writer. So it felt like I had to do something to find out whether or not there was something happening. It seemed that it was an anonymous enough process; you send it off, nobody sees you, you can sneak it into the office; and then I won the damn thing. I was a kid starting out, basically, so the quality probably wasn't very high; but for me at least it gave me that sense that maybe there was something there. That was encouragement to just keep at it.

And then the goal posts kept being moved. Five years ago, if someone had said to me: in five years you'll have published two books of poetry and a book of stories, there'd be some reviews, etc. — I would have said: You can shoot me then, because I'll die happy. Of course I don't feel that way at all now. I'm really pleased that these things have happened; but it's not enough to make me feel content.

And the blurbs are a funny thing. Every book you pick up has something on the back saying this is the greatest thing since I-don't-know-what. It starts to be meaningless. I've always been grateful that the blurbs on my books are relatively modest. That's as much as I want them to say, because they're not more than that. I think *Hard Light* is a good book, and I really enjoyed writing it. I may never write a better one; but beyond that it's not. I think it's the same with prizes. There are so many of them now that they're beginning to become meaningless. They may bring you a little more attention when you win, and maybe they'll give you some money, which is a good thing.

There are way more people in Canada who write poetry than read poetry. I'd probably never go near a poetry slam. The kind of stuff that happens at a slam has nothing to do with what interests me about poetry. I would never want to participate in one because I don't think the kind of stuff I write would be of interest to the kind of people who go to them.

I was talking to someone about [leaving Newfoundland] recently. He was talking about how a lot of Newfoundlanders who were away could not live away for long. They couldn't live away from the weather, they couldn't live away from the landscape, they couldn't live away from the people. He said he really felt that in my writing. But I don't think that's true. My attachment to the place is a very literary one. Almost everything I've written is about the place. In that sense I'm really connected to it. I don't know if I'll ever leave it. On the other hand I don't feel the same sense that I need to live here, because I miss the place that way, which is very different. I mean, Kingston is home to me now. I've been there eleven years. My closest friends are there. The people I think of as family now, who aren't my family, are all in Kingston. From the time I left I don't think I really felt that tug, that physical tug to come back here and live here again. Partly it's because I'm an out-of-sight-out-of-mind kind of guy. I've lived in homes that I've loved for years and left them and never thought about it again. A lot of my friends don't feel that way. They get really attached to a place and miss it when they move. I don't as much.

VC: *You're not one of those 1000 Newfoundlanders per month who are said to be leaving the province these days?*

MC: I never intended to leave. Beyond going to Kingston for graduate work I had no plans. By the time I quit graduate school I had met a woman, had fallen in love, and didn't really have anything to come back to, in terms of a job, so I started looking for work there. It seems like my whole life has been accidental. Wherever I've ended up, whatever I've ended up doing, it's sort of been what's been in front of me. For instance, I've never really been interested in traveling; but I've been in Central America, I've been to China. It's all been circumstantial. If the woman I was living with hadn't been on an exchange program with China I never would have lived there for a year. I loved it when I was there. I had a spectacular time. I loved the people, I loved so many of the things we saw there. But I don't really want to go back. If something fell in my lap I'd go; but otherwise ...

Sometimes I think I'm slightly autistic. I don't really know what that is about me. I don't understand it, and I'm not sure I like it. That's why I'm really grateful for writing, because that is a connection with this place. I'd feel really badly if I didn't have that. You might think this is a ridiculous comparison, but I have friends who are Jewish — they don't have anything to do with the church, they're not religious at all — but they're Jewish. They're always going to be Jewish. There are people who left Newfoundland when they were six and they're Newfoundlanders. They could be second generation New Yorkers working high steel who talk like New Yorkers, who grew up there, but when asked, they say their fathers were ship-riggers from Newfoundland. It's unlike anywhere else in Canada, I think, there's that sense of connection to this place as a distinct entity.

Newfoundland poet Michael Crummey was interviewed on September 21, 1998, by Victor Coleman and Lynn Donaghue. This interview ran in Matrix *#56.*

Gail Scott

Interviewed by **COREY FROST**

INTERTEXTS

COREY FROST: *Let's start with B: Walter Benjamin. Tell me about his influence on* My Paris.

GAIL SCOTT: Both [Gertrude] Stein and Benjamin stroll through *My Paris* as literary ghosts. Benjamin is there in a particularly intimate way, almost a friend or lover whom she calls B and whose Arcades Project [*Paris: Capitale du XIXe siècle*] she reads in bed every morning. It becomes a site map for her exploration of Paris, but more than that, the work starts to infuse her way of thinking. The Arcades Project is actually a huge pile of detritus, 19th-century quotes and anecdotes, put together in a series of montages. Benjamin was looking for a way to write a history based on found objects, juxtaposed in unexpected or contradictory ways, in order to continually challenge the biases of both the historian and the reader. The point was to make the historian, as a writing subject, not disappear but become a construction of the whole. *My Paris* isn't exactly a montage, but in a way the diary form is a montage, like it or not. It's discontinuous. Sometimes things are juxtaposed in a shocking manner. For example the action in the men's clothing shop window across from her studio on boulevard Raspail, always changing. There's almost more action in shop windows than in real life.

CF: *Those juxtapositions really struck me, like Bambi going by on the bus. They're brilliant: very disruptive of the expected trajectory of narrative. Which came first, the idea for the novel, or your interest in the Arcades Project?*

GS: Well, to answer sort of anecdotally, somebody gave me the book as a present and I went to Paris with it. And I wrote a diary, but all the time I was reading Walter Benjamin. At first I thought the diary would be a straightforward travel diary. But a so-called straightforward travel diary — there are tons of them around these days — features an essentially 19th century traveller: the One sucking up the exoticism of the Other. The old Imperialist model.

Certainly that long careful reading I did of Benjamin in Paris showed me other narrative options. As reading Stein suggests other syntactical options. But whatever is learned from Benjamin or Stein gets subsumed into the artistic needs of the late 90s diary and character. The dead authors become traces in the work, clashing with new technologies and life in the streets now, which is both the same as and very different from life in the streets when they wrote.

CF: *Had you been interested in Benjamin before?*

GS: Oh yeah. I've been reading Benjamin for a long long time, ever since I was in the Left in the 70s. He's somebody who really understood that place between Marxism and what they call the superstructure or means of production of culture, which I don't think many Marxists really understood. He understood it without having to reject Marxism altogether. Or some kind of leftist thinking, not necessarily orthodox Marxism. Benjamin's also in *Main Brides*, there are references to him. As a left person and later a feminist, I learned from writers like Benjamin and the Surrealists how to remain fluid in my thinking, to learn from these crucial movements without conceding, artistically, to the dogmatism that political movements, with their particular tasks, run the eternal risk of projecting.

CF: *What about the* flâneur. *According to Benjamin, the* flâneur *as a historical persona vanished with the advent of modernism, but continued to be a rich allegorical figure. The narrator in* My Paris *is a* flâneuse *of sorts, but doesn't feel comfortable in that role either. Do you see the* flâneur *as a useful figure for interpreting the contemporary city, or is it too problematic today?*

GS: One interesting thing in the Arcades Project is that the *flâneur* has to find a means of economic survival at some point... The first *flâneurs* in 19th-century Paris were the sons of rich men protesting Daddy's money — made on the backs of factory workers in the industrial revolution — by leaning against walls, wearing cloaks lined with scarlet. One incarnation of the *flâneur* was the dandy, who was picking up boys, mostly. The Oscar Wilde figure is a classic *flâneur*. But Benjamin points out that at a certain point the *flâneur* has to start surviving so he becomes a journalist and sells his observations; thus the *flâneur* becomes a complete mockery of what he represented in the beginning: resistance/flaunting representation of the increasing monotony of capitalism.

CF: *You can't escape economics.*

GS: Right. But I still hear people talking about *flânerie* in Paris and it just strikes me as being completely ludicrous. A professor on sabbatical, or a person on their junior year abroad, or a writer, like myself, who gets a grant to a very comfortable studio, does not represent, unless she finds some very original way to live, the spirit of resistance and enforced marginality that the early *flâneur* aimed for. The *flâneur* flaunted his sloth in an insulting manner. Another point that Benjamin makes, that then gets juxtaposed on my own text, is who are the real *flâneurs* today? In Paris they're the homeless people looking for cobblestones that aren't too bumpy to sleep on. Or the *sans papiers*, refugees. Those are the *flâneurs* today.

CF: *There are certain words from Benjamin that you fix on and use repeatedly, like "physiognomy." What does that mean for you in the text?*

GS: That's a hard question, partly because the face in the crowd is one of the things I go back to again and again in my work, without getting to the bottom. *Main Brides* might be considered, on some level, an obsession with the face of the stranger. Anyway, there is the notion that the *flâneur* collects physiognomies. And inasmuch as [the narrator] has residues of this desire to be a flâneur I guess physiognomies are one of the things that she tries to collect, except it's always so fleeting. I think some of her most successful attempts to do that are with faces she sees on TV. She certainly has a romantic idea when she gets to Paris that she's going to be this flâneur, but she just doesn't know where to go. She doesn't know how to do it. She's too timid, whimsical. Spends hours getting dressed to get lost in the crowd. Goes into cafés and looks at herself in the mirror, or looks at other people looking at themselves in the mirror, instead of actually walking around looking into faces and saying, I can tell a whole story from that face.

CF: *"Whimsical" is another resonant word. The* flâneur *is whimsical, and the narrator seems modelled on that.*

GS: Was the *flâneur* whimsical? I don't think so. I think the *flâneur* took himself very seriously. And that's precisely what she can't do.

CF: *There are references in the novel, for example, to the flâneur walking a tortoise in the arcades, and Benjamin has a quote about Nerval with a lobster on a leash. That's the kind of whimsy I'm talking about.*

GS: But I think the difference, and this is the difference between the 19th century and now, is that the *flâneur* had a kind of ironic stance, the *flâneur*'s flaunting of himself in his outfit was very ironic, and I think that's very 19th-century and it requires someone who considers themselves a fairly well-constituted subject. Whereas this character is not ironic, she's parodic. She's in a different space — and we never know whether she doesn't make it as a full subject because she doesn't know how, or if, as she implies, she's making herself minuscule, inconsequential, the better to not over-influence her story with her own subjectivity. In fact, the *flâneur* is lost in the crowd but is also in full control of his own individuality, Benjamin says. And that's different from her clownish, Chaplinesque posture. Which is far more deconstructed in a way.

CF: *More of an object than a subject?*

GS: I think she marks a place where, in interesting prose today, which is not much prose [laughing], the subject has gotten displaced—between the subject and the object as opposed to being here, with the object over there. The whimsy has to do with that.

CF: *Alright. Now GS: the review in* The Globe and Mail *calls you a Québécoise Gertrude Stein. What do you think?*

GS: Well, I think that the person writing that review of the book didn't get it. She didn't get the fact that the narrator of the book has in fact a love-hate relationship with everything Stein and the expatriates represented. On one hand she totally admires Stein's work. And I do think Stein is one of the greatest 20th-century writers. But at the same time she doesn't want to have the kind of relationship to the world around her that these people had — they seemed to be defined to some extent by what was happening in the expatriate milieu, or bounded by it. The problems of others, the economic situation of ordinary Parisians, for example, rarely comes up as an issue. [James] Baldwin, not surprisingly, was an exception. *The Globe and Mail* reviewer didn't see the parody.

CF: *What is it about Gertrude Stein's relationship to the world around her that you find problematic?*

GS: There is Stein the persona and there is the writing. We can reframe with hindsight the limitations of her vision, her republican enthusiasm. Basically, Stein noticed that the Americans, in inventing the automobile, were inventing the 20th century, but she didn't notice the Imperialist payback. I mean, the automobile is a very fraught sign for everything that was to come after. It's true: it changed our world. It changed our lives, provided us with tremendous mobility. But, will the planet be around a century from now, given the automobile? So that's not a useful trope anymore. At the same time, the way the automobile moves, and even the way it is produced, were picked up in Stein's sentences. Her ability to see how extraordinary that invention was as a defining element of her epoch helped her revolutionize narration.

CF: *Another intertext is from Balzac: the narrator's favourite Balzac heroine is* The Girl with the Golden Eyes. *Why is that character important to her?*

GS: Well, she's like that person in a way. I mean, she would love to live this cloistered life where someone else takes care of her. At the same time, the Balzac heroine has a kind of split desire: she's sequestered by the Marquise and likes that a lot but at the same time she desires the Tom who's prowling around the *Tuileries* and running after her.

CF: *She's between hetero- and homo-sexuality.*

GS: Right. And I think the character in this book, she's not bisexual by any means, but she's (a) trying to avoid categories all the time, and (b) phenomenally interested in the question of exotic beauty which for her the Balzac heroine represents.

CF: *There's a really Orientalist portrayal of her in the Balzac story. By identifying with the girl with the golden eyes, is the narrator trying to turn herself into an exotic, Orientalized object, a figure from 'the South?'*

GS: She might desire to make herself an Orientalized figure. I certainly don't think she succeeds. I think she probably does have some desire to do that.

CF: *It's interesting that there's a slippage for the Western subject from desiring that Orientalized figure to desiring to become that figure.*

GS: Right. But without any of the inconveniences of being that figure. Because she doesn't want to be deported, she doesn't want to live like the Algerians in Paris, or First Nations people here, or young Africans, whom the police see as perpetual culprits. She wants to live in her nice surroundings. I mean that's one of her contradictions — in some ways she's a very typical Western traveller.

CF: *Mmm. What about Canadians in Paris? While writing this novel, or in* *general, do you feel a connection to Canadian expats such as Mavis Gallant or John Glassco? That tradition?*

GS: Certainly not Mavis Gallant. I think she's an important writer, but I don't think she belongs to the same current in writing as I do. Wherever I go and whatever I do, I'm always looking for this thing that I think of as being about subversion, contradiction. The writer through her story telling proposes new ways of seeing. Every writer does this in some way. But some choose the more direct, witnessing end of the scale, in terms of intention. I love John Glassco's book about Paris [*Memoirs of Montparnasse*] but I don't really identify with it either. Partly because he comes from the "other Montreal" I suppose.

CF: *A colleague, Justin Edwards, pointed out to me that John Glassco constructs and perpetuates the "Lost Generation" myth without ever talking about being gay. Mavis Gallant also mythologizes Paris, and while she's never come out as a lesbian, that seems to be a submerged theme in some of her stories. My Paris is somehow similar to but the opposite of their writing in that it "outs" that experience of Paris.*

GS: Right. I would agree with that. But I also think that *My Paris* is a quest for something else that comes from a whole political tradition that I don't think either of those writers are interested in, from what I can see.

CF: *I found the way the intertexts are introduced really interesting. You refer to Walter Benjamin early on, then you start to call him B. Just as all the friends are named P, S, C, etc. That really integrates him into the social sphere. So I was wondering, while you were writing this book, how did you experience that relationship to these other texts?*

GS: The narrator, as she becomes more and more intimate with Benjamin, reduces him to B. She also provides him with a double, her friend R from Winnipeg who looks like B. But her almost porous, inconsequential persona makes her incapable of real relationships — until the coda when she redoes the whole city in a fast take as a lover.

CF: *So there's a kind of confusion between the experience of the text you're reading, the Benjamin text, and the experience of the "real" people.*

GS: Oh absolutely. In that respect I think the Paris she experiences is very much a text. But then I think probably everything is text. Except sex maybe.

TRAVEL

CF: *I was thinking that all of your novels are some kind of travel writing.*

GS: Nobody's ever said that to me before! They're always saying, oh the narrator's so stationary, she's either lying in a tub or sitting in a bar...

CF: No, but it's true. Take the protagonist in *Heroine*: She arrives in Montréal from elsewhere, in search of a new experience of self. And although it becomes her home, it's very much a site of exploration for her, and a means of escape. She lives in the Waikiki Tourist Rooms, after all. In *Main Brides*, there's a lot of travel: at least in the portraits she continually imagines herself elsewhere.

GS: *That's true. I never thought of that before.*

CF: *Your new novel, though, is the most specifically a travel story. Why did you choose Paris as a destination?*

GS: Well, first of all it was the luck of the draw because I won this studio. The leisure-lottery studio, her friends called it. But Paris for many many reasons. First of all, I think Paris belongs to the Western world. I mean you can't look at Western 20th-century literature — until the advent of post-colonialism and the rise of minority culture writing — and not trace it directly or indirectly, to something that happened in France — the Surrealists, New Wave film, post-structuralism etc., May '68 was phenomenally important, Kurt Schwitters, all that stuff. So Paris in Western culture is huge. To me it makes a lot of sense to go there. London doesn't do that for me personally. I just don't see another single city like Paris in terms of being able to look back at the century and see what's happened in the "tradition" of white avant-garde writing.

CF: *So you feel a part of the Western tradition that is centred in Paris ...*

GS: I feel a part of the, for want of a better word, avant-garde tradition (that's an oxymoron), which has roots in Paris. I don't think it's centred in Paris anymore. Paris is too expensive to produce the kind of easy-going excitement that the great exchange rates produced for writers in the 30s and 40s. That's why you're in Montreal now, right?

CF: *Right. It's cheap. That's one reason. In the book, though, the narrator doesn't really come in contact with those roots that she's ostensibly looking for.*

GS: No, she doesn't. Well, she does between the covers of books and in occa-sional conversations. I mean, she can walk through the neighbourhood. She lives in one of the neighbourhoods that Proust lived in. Right around the cor-ner from Gertrude Stein. Joyce lived half a block down. So she's kind of sur-rounded. At the same time, contemporary Paris, with its huge minority com-munities, and the endless influx of refugees, upsets the romantic notions of Paris completely, including the notion implicit in the word "roots." That's the weird thing about Paris. It's completely packed with history, beauty, memo-ries, references, all the time. And yet, as in all major metropolises, survival is really the outstanding issue.

CF: *According to the mayor quoted in the novel you need at least $4,000 a month to live there.*

GS: Yeah. Even then. I mean, part of her thing about going to Paris, because she's gay, is that she wants to find her "women of the left bank." And who were they in the 20s or the 30s? They were people who had tons of money or had friends who had tons of money. None of the women she meets on the left bank have two cents to rub together. They're all, virtually, blue-collar workers. Most of them have been through various struggles, various left-wing struggles — in Paris some women still walk around in peaked caps! It's just not the Paris of expatriate writing any more at all.

CF: *One aspect of the travel experience in the novel is constant paranoia. The imperative of passing as a native, as a Parisian. Do you think that's a uni-versal feature of travel, or is it a part of the post-colonial, centre-periphery dynamic? Does going to Paris from Canada involve searching for colonial roots?*

GS: I think, for one thing, she makes it very clear in the book that she's not authentic Québécoise. So she's not searching for roots in the way a total fran-cophone would be searching for roots and for whom that's no joke because it's the one place on Earth that nourishes the language of the francophonie — nourishes and at the same time mocks writing/language from the so-called margins. But that culture is necessary for the survival of this Québécois culture. She's presented as a kind of half-and-half person who is looking more for a literary tradition than she is for a language. The post-colonial thing — I wanted to play a little bit with the whole business of being Canadian and trav-elling. I remember when I was a student and travelling in Eastern Europe, I naively thought people would be nice to me when they learned I was from

Canada. But they just said, oh, like America! And I protested. No! No! But the Canadian thing is so contradictory. First of all it's this business of being a non-nation that can't seem to coalesce into what a republic represents. What is a republic? The French Revolution, for example, was in theory about equalizing subjects, protecting them so that each person could stand as an individual in Liberty, Fraternity, whatever.

CF: *The preservation of our Western concept of individuality, essentially.*

GS: Exactly. In Canada we buy into that and at the same time we pretend we don't. On the one hand we're the vertical mosaic and on the other there's this constant struggle for the dominance of one culture over another. Canadian history just crawls with appalling incidents of that. So how does an anglo-Québécoise situate herself in travel? I saw this person as having a literary mission, a writing mission. So the place she could situate herself was in sentences. Not anywhere else.

CF: *Not in a nationality certainly.*

GS: No. So then the question is what kind of sentences. Which is why there's this constant examination of Stein's sentences with their big subject sucking up all the action generated by predicates. Again, Gertrude Stein said that the sentences were kind of like automobiles going across a landscape. So here's this other person who comes not only from Canada but from Québec. You know: the whole question of nation-state, complete disaster. And in Québec even more than in the rest of Canada there is a strong republican desire. On one hand she's appalled that it takes so much military hardware to prop up this notion of the individual — which we don't see in Canada, everyone knows that our military is a joke — and on the other hand she's very wary of creating, in her writing, the strongly bounded subject which in a sense is the literary equivalent of republicanism. So she's looking for something else. And that's why her sentences get smaller and smaller. With present participles which are kind of a way of looking backwards and forwards at the same time but not necessarily going anywhere. Maybe it's in answer to that *Globe and Mail* review [by Stan Persky, of *Main Brides*] which said, you know, there's no action in this novel. So here I invented a sentence where, really, nothing happens. I think that the desire to make herself small enough to take in the world in a way that she considers acceptable as a traveller — to get back to the post-colonial thing — acknowledges her own failures and her country's failures to be non-racist. She somehow thinks if she can make herself small and porous enough she'll be able to empathize with everything, every aspect of life in contemporary Paris. Maybe find a different way to narrate this. At the same time, she's aware of the impossibility and hypocrisy of her own situation. Because while she tries to become smaller and more absorbant, eventually she ceases to exist as a person. And the less bounded she tries to be, the more paranoid she gets. She never gets laid in Paris, not the first trip. And when she returns with a lover, she doesn't see the city. It's all fogged in. As if she can't find her place as a subject. And in this book, the difficulty of achieving subject status has little to do with feminism. I mean I've learned things from feminism that I've applied, but here the focus is not feminism at all.

CF: *Hm. It surprises me to hear you say that. But we'll get to that in a few minutes. I want to ask you more about republicanism. At first I thought the observations about republicans were incidental, but then I realized that in fact republicanism is fundamental to neo-Imperialism. Could the drive to assert one's individuality — one's sovereignty — ultimately lead to Imperialism?*

GS: Well that seems to be the contemporary version but don't forget that some of the greatest Imperialists of all were the Brits. Contemporaneously, there is no doubt that America rules the world. Small-r republicanism, which she refers to in the novel when she talks about Benjamin talking about Poe's "Man of the Crowd" — the dangers of a notion of Equality where everyone is the same — is a metaphor for the endless thrust of the Imperial power towards hegemony of ideas and culture. But then, since there's always a contradiction, if you look at the United States, it's remarkably multi-cultural, increasingly so. Developments that perhaps point to the new millennium.

CF: *If America or France as republics have this government-sanctioned sense of individuality, a unified self, does that make Canada, as a nonnational country without the same unified identity, a more suitable place for writing a de-centred, post-modern subject? Or is that just an excuse for finding our own sort of agency in post-modernism?*

GS: Or the whatever-comes-after-post-modern. Well, one would like to think it might. So far, there is not a lot of evidence for that in the Canadian novel. I think Canadians have a very fraught relationship with this stuff. I mean the narrator talks sometimes about how she likes the present participle because she can look backwards and look forwards at the same time. But she has problems staying in the present. She's always got one foot in the 19th century. And hopefully one in the 21st. In Canada, we haven't had a bourgeois revolution.

We missed that stage somehow. Unfortunately, instead of looking forward to new possibilities, we are hopelessly nostalgic for some kind of dominance of a "national dream" that only suits part of the population: not Québec; not First Nations people, among others.

CF: *That's why you say Canada has a 19th-century mentality.*

GS: Yes. But in a way what I'm trying to say in the book is: all you can do is put little things together. You can't come up with big answers. So as soon as she puts something together she finds another element that contradicts that, and that changes what came before and what comes after. A huge puzzle ...

ANTI-TRAVEL

CF: *One curious thing in the novel is the way you use bold typefaces. All the place names, for example, the cafés, the famous buildings, the legendary bars, are in bold — in other words it's dressed up like a travel guide. But it's also antithetical to that. Is that a comment on travel guides, or travel in general?*

GS: Well, in a way it could be a travel guide, I think. I mean it won't turn up anything fantastically exciting. A café here, a café there. But actually with the bold text I was also thinking of old surrealist books which would occasionally put words in bold. Often in documents from that period people would put, not necessarily place names, but various things in bold. Because they were very interested in signs. It over-emphasizes that words are just signs, everything is a sign. So the signs that are literally signs, the place names, get to be signed twice.

CF: *It's funny because the premise of a travel guide is that a travel experience can be replicated. That one person can write about their trip, and then another person can read it and, by following the instructions, have a similar experience. Whereas the novel is so much about not having the experience you expected. I mean, Benjamin attempted to write a history in montage in order to disrupt linear thinking, but you took his history as a kind of travel guide. And because this guide is so disconnected, so aleatory, it disrupts the narrative of travel, the idea of travel as a story that can be re-lived by others.*

GS: Well, it kind of raises the problem of direct representation, which we know from reading old travel guides — and you and Dana [Bath] know from the work you've been doing with travel writing — is incredibly problematic. I think one reason it took me so long to write this book was that I had to find a way to write it that really evacuated (to use a Gallicism) as much as possible that issue of who speaks. Travel writing can never be representational. You know, the best travel book I ever read, I can't remember the name of it, but it's by a British woman who rides a horse through the mountains of Andalusia, and the whole book is about her relationship with this old nag that she got cheated on when she bought it somewhere in Spain. It's perfect.

CF: *That would be a perfect example of anti-travel writing, in my under-standing. Where it's not about the Imperial subject sopping up observations of the exotic landscape, it's about the traveller's subjecthood intersecting with other subjects, or being called into question. Does the phrase anti-travel writing mean anything to you? Is it a phrase you would apply to* My Paris?

GS: Well, I don't know if my book is anti-travel writing. I think I try to avoid naming extremes, you know. I don't want it to be this, that, or the other thing so much as to profoundly question what the whole activity might be. Could be. Anti implies that there's a For. I did want to do something different than trav-el writing. In the beginning, these little funny sentences started to creep in. And I thought, now look Gail. For once in your life you've got a book that's maybe going to make you some money. Don't spoil it! And the more I tried not to, the more these sentences crept in. I kept showing it to people and saying, do you think I can use these?

CF: *And the more you thought about it the more you couldn't resist the impulse to spoil it.*

GS: Spoil in the sense of using unusual grammar, grammar that questions the subject/object relationship in the sentence — as a conduit for questioning the same relationship in travel writing. Ultimately it's more satisfactory, for me — and, I hope, the reader. So that's what happened. In the studio, she travels as much on TV as she does in the city of Paris. Which she already thinks she knows from all the books she's read, all the TV programmes, all the movies. So one of the issues is, if people travel to have experiences, well, experiences are not that easy to have, especially in a place like Paris that's been so mythol-ogized already. I experience Paris more like techno music or something — coming at you all over the place. And for me the whole question in writing *My Paris* was how to put the writing subject in a posture that would allow her to take in the city as densely as possible and at the same time juxtapose that against her hackneyed ideas, expectations, and very privileged white Westerner travel possibilities, you know, that other people don't have. She's walking around aware that people without papers are trying to not get thrown out of the country, because they've escaped from some war somewhere in Africa, or from Eastern Europe. People are jumping into the Seine because they don't have the proper identity papers or they're hiding behind posts in the subway at 5:30 in the morning while they sneak off to their under-paid exploitative job. So I mean, what is a traveller today? Who is a traveller?

CF: *In the interview with Diana Tegenkamp, you said that the narrator of* My Paris *is not a real nomad. Deleuze and Guattari's notion of deterritorial-ization, as a linguistic shift rather than a geographic one, seems more apt. Does she go to Paris in order to experience a linguistic deterritorialization?*

GS: I'll read you something I wrote about deterritorialization: She is barely more deterritorialized than she is at home. The city is strange but so is what she sees on TV — the substitute for Sherlock Holmes' 19th-century fire. Nomadism isn't really about travelling. The exotic and new experience is get-ting harder and harder to find. The question here is more about how we are in relationship to community, country, gender, world. Something is breaking down. Identity is becoming a parody of itself as people drift and merge in new cultures. Virilio says the real nomads in the 21st century will be the poor, the people without countries, etc. We already see this in cities like Paris. The rich will stay home or go to outer space on vacation. Totally equipped and outfit-ted. Which I guess gets one out of the nomad category.

CF: *Is it possible to be a nomad within your own language?*

GS: For me, a place like Paris permits me to be somewhat of a nomad in my own language, just as Québec does. But even this is mediated by so much speaking and reading and living in French. In Paris people just laugh their heads off at my accent. At first they think I'm Québecoise and they adopt this really sympathetic posture, then English comes out invariably and they don't know what to do.

CF: *It's a sympathetic reaction to the Québécois accent? Not patronizing?*

GS: Well, maybe patronizing but sympathetic. But it's hard for them to be sympathetic to an English accent, when English is the boss of the world. So it puts them in a real weird situation and me too. But that Deleuzian notion of deterritorialization is really at play in the way French affects my English. Even the use of verbs — participles don't work really in French, but — the idea that

English tends to be a far more descriptive language, while French is more intervening. I think nobody has ever looked at this in Stein and it would be interesting if they did: how the influence of living in Paris made her focus so much on verbs in writing English.

CF: *Stein did talk about how being in Paris allowed her language to change because it was in isolation.*

GS: But that's the interesting thing about the expatriates of that period: that they did think of themselves as isolated. That's impossible today, for us. I don't think we can live like that anymore.

CF: *Does that problematize the comparison between those expats in Paris and, for example, English Canadians coming to live in Montréal?*

GS: I think yes and no. Being Canadian or being in Canada gives us a very conflicted and hypocritical relationship, historically speaking, towards the French language. Most people who come here already have some background in French; simultaneously, there is a malaise around language that signals all is not right, which comes from a fundamental dichotomy in Canadian history. Is there a guilt factor involved? Must one either feel guilty or closed off? So, you see, it's not quite the same thing.

CF: *For English Canadians who come here, I think there's a general feeling that you're not fully experiencing life in Montréal unless you're integrated somewhat into the French-speaking community. Although most of us fail or succeed at that in varying degrees. But the "Lost Generation" in Paris, a lot of them never learned any French — Stein for example — and took a certain pride in that. There's that quote from Stein that "foreigners should be foreigners" — that there's no point in being there if you're going to go native, so to speak.*

GS: Right. Also there's a whole question of consciousness, awareness, that marks books about other places from any epoch. I think in the 19th-century travelogue, for example, the point was to go to the most exotic place possible and to bring back as many exotic objects as possible. It implies a kind of Imperialist self-other relationship that I think is muted today by the fact that, first of all, we come from such mixed backgrounds ourselves, most of us, but also because we live in a time when people are talking about post-colonialism. You can't ignore that when you're writing a book about travel. In the big cities of the world today the Imperialist chickens are coming home to roost as it were. People of former colonies — whose countries the West has destroyed by creating false boundaries so that they're in constant strife — have totally transformed the face of Western cities.

CF: *Is there a sense in which the exotic, as a concept, has lost its meaning?*

GS: I think when it pops up it's extremely suspect. That doesn't mean we're not all prey to it. In some ways we still have that desire. Part of her big disappointment about being in Paris is the Paris she's missing, that she keeps talking about and just can't find. On one hand, it's the Paris she read about in literature departments; on the other, it's the very contemporaneous one, with North African music and mint in the margins, as she puts it.

FEMINISM & POSTMODERNISM

GS: I'd like you to tell me why you were surprised about what I said about feminism.

CF: *Well, because I think the postcolonial themes in the book are in some sense inseparable from feminism. Also, I see the main project of the book, and what I think it really accomplishes, as finding a way beyond the feminist/ postmodernist problem. The idea that in postmodernism you have a de-centred subject, a fluid and inconstant identity, and yet feminist and postcolonial movements rely on having a stable self, an identity to defend and promote.*

GS: The strategies I've learned that I try to apply in my work are definitely strategies learned from feminist attempts to express women in language. But not all feminist writing is about having a stable self. Some of us were trying to re-situate our selves as some other kind of subject less bounded, after deconstruction, when the subject, the self, was considered dead — which we all knew wasn't true. Particularly feminists and visible minorities knew this wasn't true. But in this book, I think the subject is more queer than feminist. She's more uncertain about how she's seen in the world and how she is in the world. She distances herself from feminism, both in the Sarajevo parade and when she sees the feminist on the sidewalk fasting as a protest against rape in Sarajevo. She's not really quite there. And she walks around in this black suit which is very non-gendered in a way — it's not like a skirt and heels, it's a Charlie Chaplin suit. And I don't think the clown is very gendered. Then when she does become gendered, i.e. takes on a woman lover, in the last part, she kind of ceases to be in the world. It's like she's split into two parts, she can't do both things at once, you know.

CF: *I wasn't thinking of feminism in the sense of identity politics. Both the deconstructed self and post-colonialism have been obstacles to that kind of feminism in the last couple of decades. I see the book as a new possibility. I see it as attempting to write a way for feminism to survive postmodernism.*

GS: I agree. So often when people use the word feminist it seems to refer to identity politics and I think that the writing I'm interested in right now is as much concerned with the cusps, the threshold, the movement between individuals, cultures, expressions and possibilities of gender. Having said this, had not all the other stuff gone before I wouldn't be able to do what I'm doing now either. It's a process that's taken me from there to here.

CF: *Maybe it's the focus on the in-between that makes travel writing particularly interesting right now, because it's a way of escaping the self, and a way of finding that balance that you seem to be trying to find in the book, the balance between subject and object.*

GS: Exactly. That's a really good way of putting it.

CF: *It occurred to me that* My Paris *also ties in to some of the things written lately in which the book becomes a kind of architecture. Because this is a guide to Paris, it becomes a sort of urban-planning novel. Do you think of the novel as a way of mapping the city, or is the city just the setting?*

GS: I definitely think of it as a way of mapping the city. I did that in *Main Brides* too, where I projected the characters onto a vertical grid of the city, and I did a lot of research on the architecture and decoration of the city. I don't think it's architecture per se that I'm interested in, but I'm interested in making my work very very concrete and material. That's really important to me, and that comes out of a desire to relate everyday life to the bigger structures around it. And in *Main Brides* it was to project a place for women particularly onto that structure, to map it as a space that was feminized in a way.

CF: *Because the city is basically a structure of male control.*

GS: But Montréal's a very feminine city. It's very unaggressive for one thing.

It's low, as major cities go. It's decorated in a very florid way. It has all this architectural stuff that's completely dream-like. It's also a city — and Paris is like this too — in which private space and public space come together more. You know, like in the East End people watching the TV on the sidewalk in the summertime. The outside stairs. The way people entertain out here as opposed to having people in. Paris is like that too. And Paris is shaped like a snail as well, which is labyrinthine but a very feminine kind of shape, I think. Also the manner in which Paris is so concerned with all the details of life, it's almost domestic in a way. The incredible emphasis everywhere on food, clothes, getting your nails done and your feet done. Which applies to both sexes. So in that respect I think both Paris and Montréal have a thing that's easy for me to slip into.

CF: *Where else in the world do you want to travel and why?*

GS: There are so many places I'd like to go. The cities I've been to that I really like are the free ports of the world. I love Tangiers for instance. It's not really a free port anymore but it has that history. I'd love to go to Shanghai. New Orleans is city I adore too. For some of the same reasons. I like the cities that have a slightly illicit air about them, where all is not ruled by the work ethic. My mother's family made their living running rum — well, part of my mother's family — over the American-Canadian border. Perhaps I identify vaguely with that kind of illicitness. At least with the great stories it produces.

CF: *Is that why you're interested in Shanghai?*

GS: I don't know why. It's just an idea ... You know how you fix on places. It's still the lure of the exotic I guess. One of the few exotic places.

CF: *Any plans to go back to Paris?*

GS: No. I think I'm finished writing Paris. I mean I'll go back to visit but I kind of wrote out my obsession with Paris with this book. I don't know where it is yet, but it's somewhere else.

TECHNOLOGY

CF: *You mentioned in the HOUR interview that our experience of otherness is undermined by the effect of TV on our perception: the simulated immediacy and accessibility of the world around us. This got me thinking about* *something Stein said in* Paris France.

GS: I love that book.

CF: *She said that Paris was the home of the 20th century, for various reasons, but largely because of the French nonchalant relationship to technology, the refusal to mix technology with lifestyle. Why don't you tell me about your own relationship to technology. How does it inform or impinge upon your writing?*

GS: Ah. Well now we're into something that's very different I suppose between generations. Hmm. Stein actually went even farther than that. At some point she said or strongly implied that the Americans, in order to invent the 20th century, had to go to a very 19th century place. In terms of pace of life. Where you still could and still can go into a shop and choose between ten different kinds of butter and a hundred different cheeses. That kind of artisanal production which the French still insist on is very different from the high-tech life that we as North Americans experience in everything we do. My relationship to technology depends on what technology, I guess. I feel that I've learned an awful lot from, for example, surfing the net or whatever. Because it gives me this feeling that I never had before. We construct ourselves differently on the internet or using email than any kind of self has ever been constructed. We break ourselves up into little bits and project ourselves. People fall in love on email. It certainly has affected and continues to affect my work, but I don't think I relate to it the way someone of your generation would, or someone younger who's already doing this kind of thing in elementary school, so it really is a ... what's the Deleuzian term, an extension of the body ...

CF: *A desiring-machine?*

GS: Yeah. For my daughter's generation I suppose television was that. And she's ... how old are you?

CF: [It turns out I'm the same age as her daughter.] *It's true. Television has shaped the way I see the world in many ways. Less so with the internet, because it's new, but maybe that's what it will be for people who are kids now.*

GS: Right. And I think that has really started to affect the way we see not only who we are as humans but who we are as writing subjects. It's interesting that literary movements all through the 20th century have kind of foreseen in their writing practice what's happening now. I mean the notion of the subject breaking down started really with the Surrealists, Artaud, etc. And then deconstruction came along and everyone said, oh no! But now we realize that we're living in that world.

CF: *It's almost as if the thoughts of writers and philosophers create the pre-conditions for the next cultural shift. I mean, maybe we wouldn't have been able to even conceive of something like the internet if we hadn't gone through surrealism, deconstruction and all that.*

GS: One wonders. It's hard to do the cause and effect thing, but it seems there's got to be some kind of dialectic relationship that goes on there. But I think one's relationship to technology depends not only on what time period, but also what conditions you grow up in. Where did you grow up?

CF: *P.E.I. In the country.*

GS: Yeah. And I grew up in a small town, near Cornwall [Ontario, near the Québec border]. So we didn't grow up in the 20th century in some ways. I think many people in Canada didn't, in that respect. While a lot of other people did. Children of holocaust survivors, for example, certainly had to grow up in the 20th century. So it really depends where you come from.

CF: *Speaking of the country. Your writing has always been distanced from one of the main characteristics of Canadian writing, according to Margaret Atwood, Northrop Frye etc. I mean the connection to landscape or wilderness. Your books, except for* Spare Parts, *are all urban in setting. Is that a conscious choice for you?*

GS: It probably was a conscious choice at some time. I find that I have difficulty writing if I'm not living very intensely. For me, writing and living really go together. In that way, even though I don't belong to the "performance generation," writing has always been for me a kind of performance. I need a place where I can perform. I need the place to perform back. I've tried at various times to live in Edmonton for personal reasons, and I just couldn't write there, at least not for sustained periods. There's too much physical space, between people, basically. So I need to be in a big city, really.

NARRATIVE & GRAMMAR

CF: *You've mentioned before that the kind of writing you're doing features something you call the New Narrative subject, which is mostly written by queer writers. What is New Narrative?*

GS: Well, it's just what I've been talking about all along. I think it involves the abandonment of the beginning-middle-end kind of story in favour of all kinds of montages and juxtapositions of different types of stories in the same space. Many of the younger writers in Montréal are seemingly almost spontaneously writing what falls into my idea of New Narrative. In Robert Majzels' *City of Forgetting*, there are some new narrative qualities, such as using characters from other times — inserted, almost pasted into or onto, a present-time narrative. But queer writers basically began this movement, for the most part, maybe because it involves a displacement of the writing subject in drag, plus a refusal to look away from questions of social, political, or theoretical import. There's an explicitness and flaunting of the personal, which then of course ceases to become personal. Flaunting implies with style. Above all I'd say it involves a concern with texture and language which I don't think a more teleological narrative has, because there's a goal you have to get to. In fact, it involves a refusal of any goal. So the texture of the prose becomes extremely important again, as it is in poetry, and as it was in some 18th-century writing.

CF: *That sounds very anti-narrative. What's the relationship to narrative? Why call it "New Narrative" at all?*

GS: Well, it is narrative. I mean Stein said it. Narrative is any one thing put after any other thing. For me narrative is what makes the really interesting prose being done today different from the interesting poetry being done today. Particularly the novel form is a choice you make because you want to ask big questions. And that requires certain connections and a working out of those connections. Not towards an answer, but towards really posing the questions well. I don't think poetry can take that on in the same way — poetry does something else, that prose can't take on. I say "New Narrative" *faute de quoi dire*; I can't think of a better word. The explicitness in New Narrative about who's writing, and about questioning that writing position is important because novels today are more and more about situating ourselves in history, and our relationship to history. And to the crimes of indifference that we, and our states, and our culture, commit all the time.

CF: *You say that the role of the novel is to ask big questions, but on a grammatical level anyway, you don't ask any questions in* My Paris *because there are no question marks.*

GS: Because it's just one big question! Question marks become redundant. I would have to put one after almost every sentence I suppose.

CF: *Good point. What about commas? Basically there are no commas in the text except where they're used for translation, to separate one language from another. The comma of difference.*

GS: Right. That's part of my discussion with Stein, who says in one of her passages, I can see you all together, no matter how many there are of you in a place, and I can write a portrait of you in about three words. And for me there's a relationship between that and abolishing commas which is — and I think this is also a republican project — finding what is alike in everybody. In a way, it's the genius of republicanism. But what are we afraid of in Québec, if that portrait happens? That difference will disappear. So I play with the comma here as a sign for the cusp of translation, and protecting difference from assimilation. As opposed to abolishing it altogether.

CF: *I was unsure whether the verbs in the novel were participles or gerunds. I.e. verbs or nouns. I figure that because there are never any auxiliary verbs used with them, they're not true participles. They're sort of in between.*

GS: Yeah, they are kind of in between. They are an attempt at moving backwards and forwards at the same time in the sentence. But by definition if you're moving backwards and forwards at the same time you're staying in the same place. When Carla Harryman read the book she said, Oh, this is a book of ends of sentences. She saw it as part of the sentence being missing. It's typical of Carla to find a completely different and fresh way of seeing it.

CF: *Gertrude Stein abolished the comma from this century. If you were to abolish one punctuation mark from the next century, what would it be?*

GS: Maybe quotation marks.

CF: *That's a good idea. Why would you abolish them?*

GS: Well, for the obvious reason: we're all quoting each other all the time anyway, so why put anything in quotation marks? Also I hate long dialogue in prose. The kind of dialogue I like in prose pops forward as a performance in a text as opposed to representation of real-time speech. Which is how so many people use dialogue.

THE NEXT CENTURY

CF: *I felt it wasn't coincidental that* My Paris *was written at the end of the 20th century. There's a sense of summing up what has come before, and of dreaming the future. How is writing going to evolve in the next century?*

GS: Writing is really changing, the way it changed between the 18th and 19th centuries, and I don't understand why so few people see this. For all the reasons we've talked about, and particularly the relationship of the younger generations to technology, there is no way that the kind of novels that are still sold by the dozen and advertised ad nauseum — I mean, nobody is going to care about them. It astonishes me that this industry exists that people make such a fuss about, when it's over! I'm sure it's over. I can tell from my students that it's over. Before they even talk to me. It's just the way they are in the world and they way they write about the world.

CF: *So you don't think that in the next century there are going to be murder mystery novels and so on?*

GS: Oh yeah. But they'll be different than they are. I just think that the book itself is changing, never mind the novel, the book is changing so profoundly.

CF: *Do you have a sense in your writing that, like Stein, you are inventing the next century?*

GS: No, I don't think I'm the right generation for that. I hope my work is part of that movement, but I think the people who will invent the next century, in the sense of trends and styles, were born in the 1970s and 1980s, people who are dealing with new technology, gender, race, in ways that are so interesting. Actually, I have trouble speaking of history in a linear way. I would say that the way some of us have always been writing in the last quarter of the 20th century are elements in a field just now starting to really blossom.

CF: *You said before that you think postmodernism is dead. Do you think that something else is being created to replace it, in terms of writing?*

GS: Yes, I do. I think that's a question you can almost answer better than I can, you know. I think this little Montréal scene of writers we have, our little enclave, is really interesting. Marta Cooper said to me once, it's so bizarre that the writers who are kind of our elders don't have any weight — I mean we're not the Atwoods and Ondaatjes. The good side of that is that we learn an awful lot from each other all the time. It's not like a mentor-protégé situation. Or maybe because we're a small community, there's an ongoing discussion that happens on some level.

CF: *Well, I think it's also that the Montréal writers I think of as mentors, including yourself, are much closer to what I want to be doing than the writers with mainstream clout.*

GS: But getting back to your question. There's a way that younger writers in this scene — people just starting to write — are using narrative, that kind of absorbs what has gone before in a very different way than the way somebody like myself uses narrative. But it's important that it's absorbed. I mean it doesn't "evacuate" the writing that has gone before, but absorbs it in a different way and projects something else. I find that really interesting. And while you're doing that, learning maybe from something I've done, I'm also learning from what you're doing as a generation. The generational differences are definitely there in all kinds of ways, but I think it's possible to learn from each other.

CF: *It's hard for me to think of writing like yours, or for example Kathy Acker, as something that has gone before. It's actually what I'm immersed in as a reader. It feels very connected to contemporary life, and that's why I feel much closer to it than more mainstream, representational writing. Like we were saying, the writing seems to precede the culture or mentality. The way I perceive the world today, having grown up with certain technologies, is reflected in work that Kathy Acker was doing in the 70s, or in your work.*

GS: Yeah. Kathy Acker. What a life.

CF: *Do you have any resolutions for the new millennium?*

GS: I guess just the desire to keep changing with time would be my personal resolution.

CF: *I really liked that quote from Benjamin in the book, about the danger of things staying the way they are.*

GS: Yeah. I love that too. *Que les choses continuent comme avant: voilà la catastrophe.*

Corey Frost interviewed Gail Scott in a Mile-End café for Matrix 54 *(Travel Documents Issue). At the time Corey Frost was a graduate student in* Études anglaises *at l'Université de Montréal.*

Robert Majzels

Interviewed by **LIANNE MOYES**

This could be what a conversation is — simply the outline of a becoming.
(Gilles Deleuze and Claire Parnet, Dialogues*)*

LIANNE MOYES: *In coming up with a title for your second novel, I know you proposed "Homeless in Tutonaguy" and I remember a collaborative performance with Montreal multi-media artist Gail Bourgeois in 1993 entitled "Crossing Tutonaguy." Can you tell me a bit about Tutonaguy and how it figures in your writing?*

ROBERT MAJZELS: Tutonaguy is the name which the Iroquois, the Mohawks gave to the village which was on the site where Montreal is now, the village discovered by Cartier. When Cartier arrrived he heard the name Hochelaga, a name which actually referred to the region surrounding Montreal. So he misnamed the place Hochelaga — in the usual European way. They misnamed everything. Tutonaguy was interesting to me because it can't entirely be called an Iroquois village. It was a meeting place between the Huron, the Iroquois and the Algonquin who came to trade there. The reason the village was there when Cartier first arrived and not when he returned is that it existed only during periods of exchange between the different nations. When there was a war or when there was no trade going on the village would disappear; it was a kind of line of meeting among nations. I also found it interesting that Montreal is built in layers. The book is constructed in that way. The characters go underground into the subway; there's the archaeological dig in Old Montreal where de Maisonneuve is holed up during the winter; and there is Tutonaguy. So I'm playing with space and time and history.

LM: *Montreal, then, is a place of histories written on top of other histories. Like a palimpsest.*

RM: Yes, it's a palimpsest or what Lyotard calls the clash of incommensurable spaces and times — which is what interests me: these various times that don't mesh together but which exist in the same place. They're layered and they come up to the surface no matter how much you forget them. So as he walks through the streets, de Maisonneuve hears the voices of the original inhabitants. He struggles not to hear them but he hears them nonetheless.

LM: *The title you ended up with,* City of Forgetting, *does it have anything to do with this effect of layering, with the fact that in urban space we forget very quickly what were're standing on, who previously inhabited the building or the streets? Often, we don't even ask the question.*

RM: Yes, we appropriate. We forget context and we forget history. I think it's the Arab writer Amin Malouf who said that what characterizes the West is that it has no memory; it forgets. The West will do terrible things to people for centuries and then 50 years later will turn around and wonder: why is there terrorism, why is there fundamentalism, why are the people so upset? And it's a similar thing here on our own terrain. History for us is a sequence of moments. We're at this moment now and the moment before is gone. But in fact it's not gone. It is in the future. It is always ahead of us in some way. So forgetting for me is that mistake we make. But it's also a defense. Look at Suzy Creamcheez: she forgets herself and forgetting herself is a way of getting away from the identity imposed on her, from the roles she's intended to play. So forgetting is an ambiguous thing for me; it's a form of resistance but it's also a form of oppression. On the one hand, never forget; on the other, for change to occur we must forget our selves.

LM: *You mentioned in a piece you wrote for* Matrix #49 *that the exhaustion of the great narratives of modernity is more apparent, more palpable in Montreal. In what sense? How does this exhaustion shape the novel?*

RM: That's probably a very personal point of view. But I think there are possibilities for its being more apparent.

LM: *For reading it here.*

RM: Yes, for reading it. Or maybe this is just the place I happen to be and so I read it here.

LM: *There are a lot of empty spaces in Montreal: vacant lots, empty stores, abandoned warehouses. It is less easy to make the place and its history cohere.*

RM: I was in Vancouver recently. There's a city that is filling, filling constantly, overflowing. It has its own interesting interconnections because of the influx from Asia; Vancouver is becoming an Asian city in a really interesting way. But it's not in decline. I remember saying to someone — and it horrified them — that I'm really happy to be living in a city in decline. I love the idea that Montreal is emptying out. There is so much space to move around in and rents are cheap. Young visual artists, for example, who have no entry into galleries can just rent a space and show their work. So that's one way Montreal opens up the possibility of reading the exhaustion of grand narratives. Another way is the conflict of cultures. You have all these cultures and each has struggled for many years to make up its own story of Montreal. If you listen, you can hear these stories clashing. That makes it easy not to believe in any of them and to think about the contrasts, the differences, without being above them all or washing your hands of them. You're more wary of the grand narratives that would explain the situation of Quebec one way or another.

LM: *As founder of Montreal, a character like de Maisonneuve has a direct link to the city and its history. Jeanne Mance, too, the novel suggests. I was wondering about the role of characters such as Clytemnestra, Le Corbusier, Ché Guevara, Rudolf Valentino, Lady Macbeth. What do the histories they ask us to remember have to do with contemporary Montreal?*

RM: I might approach that question in terms of how I came to each of those characters. It's very much a process of condensation or dreamwork in the way that I hit on one which will lead to something else. Why Le Corbusier? Because I'm interested in modernism, in the modernist view of time and space and subjectivity. I'm also interested in the city, in the architecture of the city. I put de Maisonneuve in the Old Port in an archaeological dig and then he sees the great grain elevaters. And in fact Le Corbusier did come to Montreal and did comment on those elevators. And so I have Le Corbusier in the city. He takes on meaning for me not as a character or as an allegorical figure but as a text, as a text made up of all these interconnecting texts. And then I came to Guevara. The original idea came to me in a guerilla zone in the Philippines when I was still writing my first novel. I was sitting one evening on a little hill above where people were cooking under a plastic cover. I was suddenly struck: here I am looking at an exhausted revolution. I had been there long enough to know. It had started with the best of intentions and terrible things had happened to it. People were dying of malaria, of tuberculosis, of other diseases. People were exhausted theoretically, philosophically. But they/we were stuck; we couldn't come down. And I realized: this is the kind of site I want to explore: on a mountaintop, isolated, burned out, witnessing the end of a great discourse, a great narrative of emancipation and wondering what we do now, how we resist now.

LM: *That reminds me of Clytemnestra on the mountaintop looking out. How does she fit?*

RM: Well, I happened to be reading Aeschylus around the time I was working on the novel. I was struck by that incredible debate about the culpability of Orestes versus that of Clytemnestra. The Gods come down on the side of Orestes, Apollo arguing that the mother merely carries the man's child. Therefore, Orestes owes his loyalty to his murdered father Agamemnon, and not to his mother Clytemnestra. Her killing Agamemnon, which she does to avenge his sacrificing of their daughter Iphigenia, is unpardonable. On these grounds Orestes' murder of his mother is pardoned. Nevertheless, Clytemnestra ruled for a time after she assassinated her husband Agamemnon. In that sense, she's the first great radical feminist and her defeat is the return of the rule of men and the establishment of the Athenian order. What the whole *Oresteia* symbolizes is the passage of the rule of the polis from the hands of the Gods to those of man. There is a moment of hysterical fear that power might fall into the hands of women. I read the play as a desparate attempt to argue why society cannot be ruled in a feminine way. Feminism is another of the great narratives of emancipation and it too has reached a point of exhaustion, a point at which it is asking a lot of questions of itself. Lady Macbeth is another woman we've been taught to hate; she's interesting because she doesn't wield the knife herself; she pushes her husband to do it. So it's more a bourgeois feminism.

When I started out, many of these characters — Clytemnestra and Lady Macbeth a bit less — were to me ridiculous, pompous: de Maisonneuve with his religious fervour or Le Corbusier with his great schemes for universal measurement, for mass housing and cities rebuilt in straight lines, schemes which have created so many disasters. But as you work on these characters, you start to see the lines of resistance and you gain respect and a certain fondness for them. So each of the characters comes in a different way. Writing is a process similar to the work of dreaming. You jump from point A to point C. It's a rhizomatic process which, unfortunately, you are taught in school to repress.

LM: *In some ways, then, when I asked about direct links between the characters and Montreal, I missed the point. The point is more that you have these characters inhabiting space simultaneously. They don't need to have a* *direct link to the city; they have a link to a moment when all of their grand solutions need to be questioned. It becomes interesting to bring them together on the international stage that is Montreal.*

RM: Yes, Montreal is also Aulis and it's Greece. Montreal exists underneath Tutonaguy. Or maybe between Tutonaguy and Cartier there is Greece. Ancient Greece wasn't actually in the space of Montreal but it's there in time. So time, space, matter, energy — they are all interrelated in ways that make it impossible to look at a thin column of geological study and say what happened here. You have to include history. But if I have to, I can argue that each of these characters has some link to Montreal. Valentino did come and dance the tango, and he did speak to the public in French and got huge applause. And Le Corbusier visited. I didn't know about the link when I was writing but it turns out that he designed dresses for women based on those Isadora Duncan had made when she was dancing. Her dresses were based on Greek dresses. In fact when I was studying Duncan, I saw a picture of her in front of the Parthenon in one of her dresses dancing. So there's a link between Clytemnestra and Le Corbusier and Duncan, all there. When you're writing and you're looking for things, all kinds of combinations surface.

LM: *What is behind the strategy of reincarnating characters as contemporary figures from the streets of Montreal, figures we are familiar with: the woman who plays the harmonica on Prince Arthur or the man who travels on a tricycle with a dog, a cat and a whole rack of prints and paintings?*

RM: That's interesting. In a review, I think, someone said that I had made the homeless people in Montreal crazy, that they imagined that they were these historical characters.

LM: *They were all deluded.*

RM: Exactly. You can come at the question from various angles. When I was thinking about revolutionary figures — and of course about Ché Guevara who is the quintessential revolutionary, the one who never compromises — I realized that I have my own mountain, so rather than setting the book in the mountains of Bolivia, I put it here. Then I asked myself what these figures would be doing if they were in Montreal today. I came to the conclusion that they would be homeless. There would be no place for them. Le Corbusier would not be received in the offices of Place Ville Marie. No one wants to hear his schemes, to hear de Maisonneuve's resistance to commercialism or

Guevara's revolution or Cytemnestra's anti-masculinism. These are discourses which have no place. So they are homeless in the city. Once I realized that, I produced the homelessness. But the homeless are real people and if you write about homeless people you face the difficulty of doing it without objectifying them. I did not want to escape that problem. I wanted to indicate it. Tying them to real people is a way of indicating that homelessness is not an abstract idea, that I recognize that I am appropriating a condition which is real, physical and horrible in our city. At the same time, I didn't want to write a kind of liberal humanist novel about poor homeless people struggling in the city and courageously resisting — or not. So I was trying to wrestle with the contradictions without escaping, denying or resolving them. This is always a challenge in writing about issues such as gender or class or race. And there's no way not to write about these issues.

LM: *On one level, giving the names of queens, celebrities, heroes to homeless people in Montreal emphasizes how the mighty are fallen. Not only are the characters' narratives exhausted but the characters themselves are old, they're ill. In some cases, they figure the backruptcy of their own ideas. They remind us how twentieth-century dreams have failed to solve basic problems like shelter. On another level, does giving those names to homeless people in Montreal not ask us to pay some attention to them, to their lives, their visions, their language?*

RM: Yes, that's another way of putting it, probably a better way. They are simultaneously the bankruptcy of the grand narratives and the attention to the people who are homeless today, to these figures who are almost part of our landscape, to these figures we don't hear.

LM: *Are they the potential revolutionaries of today?*

RM: Yes, there's potential for resistance. In the harmonica lady, I hear resistance in the way she plays. I hear resistance that I don't hear for instance in the chorus of homeless men that was created recently in Montreal. There's also resistance in her language. She talks in ways that are hard to understand. It's as hard for me to understand when she talks as it is for me to read Derrida. There's resistance to shelters, to all the institutional structures that are there to integrate the homeless into society. But I'm not romanticizing their situation either. They suffer terribly. We have no institutions capable of helping them. We have failed to create a society that could help them. And we feel it when we're confronted with them. The homeless person is the Other in the land of plenty. When I turn my gaze on a homeless person, I see my past and, very possibly, my future.

LM: *The problem of shelter is nowhere more evident than in the case of the character Le Corbusier who writes a letter requesting an audience with Rockefeller but is unable to give a return address. The book has some wonderfully funny moments and I wondered about the role of humour — in keeping the contradictions in play.*

RM: The humour in this novel, even more than in the first one, is very dark.

LM: *It often comes from really radical ironies.*

RM: Yes. For me, humour is a form of resistance — in a Bakhtinian sense. It is a way of undermining authority. So just when you think you're saying something profoundly true and evident, you suddenly feel the carpet slipping out from under you. I don't do it on purpose but it keeps happening. I keep finding these moments: he wouldn't of course have a return address, I realize as I'm finishing the letter. I try to integrate those moments.

LM: *Within the novel, there is a positive side to the movement, the wandering, the refusal of codified, solidified existence. This leads me to my next question about Jewishness. The novel doesn't take up Jewishness in an explicit way, but I couldn't help thinking about your comments in that article in* Matrix *about a kind of Jewishness which is neither exclusive nor common to all Jews, about an inter-national nation, a non-national nation, about viscosity.*

RM: The slime factor, I call it.

LM: *Yes, and I wondered — straddling borders, confusing identities, mobility, fluids, bodily fluids, meteorological fluids — are these part of the novel's oblique relation to Jewishness? How would you articulate that relation?*

RM: It's part of the debate over Jewishness that's been around for a long time: diaspora versus Zionism. And obviously, I'm more sympathetic to the diaspora position because I see in that terrible situation of being homeless the possibility for resistance. It's an ethical position for me. You can't keep your hands entirely clean if you live in this world but you can certainly resist as much as possible the power that tempts and is offered to you as male, as white. And Jewishness, to me, is an opportunity — at the same time that it's a curse — an opportunity for that resistance. The homelessness of Jewishness, or the homelessness of homelessness, is a situation of movement, of sliding, of liquidity that offers a possible avenue for resistance. Once the strategies of revolution and social change have collapsed, what we have are the possibilities for tactics and for temporary alliances. I ended my first novel on that idea of the temporary. The novel ends with the women taking over the asylum, but temporarily, and aligning themselves with some of the men and with women from different races and classes. So these alliances can occur and dissolve and restructure, but there's a constant shifting of identity and self: breaking down and rebuilding and staying on your toes to catch the possibilities at all times.

LM: *In the way that the characters do. They're creating alliances. They're also staying on their toes.*

RM: That's right. They don't trust each other. They lie at moments.

LM: *They pick each others' pockets.*

RM: They pick each others' pockets when necessary. Clytemnestra knows that as a woman there's just so much she's going to be able to trust any man. And even between her and Lady Macbeth, there's only so much alliance possible. There are differences and these differences are not denied. There are no totalizing strategies possible, but there are tactics of resistance which necessarily imply fluidity, movement, shifts. For me, Jewishness is one way of describing that, homelessness is another.

LM: *It would be difficult to talk about* City of Forgetting *without talking about intertextuality. Certainly some reviewers have worried about the number of citations and the difficulty of distinguishing them from your words. What does it mean to you to cite other texts?*

RM: Well, the right way to write this novel would have been to bury all the intertextuality in the form of allusion. I wanted to bring to the surface what is usually buried, to take away from academics the pleasure of doing all that work. My book is no more intertextual than any other book I've ever read. It's just that I've made the seams visible, I've shown people where I sewed in the references. Unconsciously, that's how we write. We write out of the texts we've read, not out of creation. We're not Gods. We don't invent anything. We condense things. That to me is the point of the book. It's about reading as a form of struggle and a relation of power. Any book is made up of other books just as any person is made up of all these texts. I am no more a real person than Clytemnestra, Guevara, or Suzy. That's what interests me about writing today. If people see that as a problem, it's likely that they are looking for my own unique personal voice, the humanist concept of the speaking subject as a source of meaning. I wanted to problematize the concept of the author, and the person.

LM: *The range of texts referred to is incredible. There's everything from* The Jesuit Relations *to Mohawk phrases to Mao Zedong. This range disrupts the modernist reliance on the Western tradition.*

RM: An important point. No one I know who has read the novel is familiar with all those texts. So in a way, the text cuts through the structure of knowledge we're supposed to have. If we repeat that structure, we reproduce the Western subject as we know it. By introducing texts that are not supposed to be part of it, we disrupt that Western subject and open it up to other possibilities. Hence the Mohawk texts — which were tough because I had to find them and I had to go to Kahnawake to get Mohawks to help me with the spelling. It was another struggle, a totally different struggle, to get the Greek stuff right.

LM: *And it probably involved going to different places.*

RM: Exactly. And when you want Mao, you go to another place that isn't in the academy at all; it isn't even in the Marxist academy because he's Chinese and he doesn't have a voice in the academy. For me, intertextuality is crucial to the novel. One of the things I was told by a publisher who refused the novel originally is that I could solve the problem if I would just give the characters names like George, Henry, Mabel and let the reader discover who they are instead of, as the publisher put it "making the reader feel inadequate." When I read something I like, I do have a sense of inadequacy — which drives me back to the library. And that's what I want to do in my writing. I don't have to teach anybody anything; I just have to respond to things and let others respond.

LM: *The absence of footnotes in the body of the text gives the effect of seamlessness at the same time that the reader hears echoes of other texts. Why did you choose to omit the notes?*

RM: Everybody recognizes something. Let's say you're reading and you know Lorca and you see a reference that you recognize. You flip to the back and the scene breaks there. Somebody else doesn't know Lorca but they know Le Corbusier or Lady Macbeth, so their reading is disrupted somewhere else. I didn't want to put footnotes in the text. I wanted the problem of references, the disturbing aspect. The solution I found works, I hope, because it makes a problem of reference without being an actual plagiarism. And it has disturbed people. But unfortunately, so few reviewers, when they're disturbed, think about it.

LM: *Is it a coincidence that the fictional characters in the novel are women and the historical characters are men?*

RM: That's a very good question. That happened originally entirely by accident. And it was pointed out to me by Gail Bourgeois when I was beginning to write the text. I was working on the text and she was working with video, photographs and drawings. And we were just sort of clashing and seeing what was happening. At one point, she said to me "Look, your characters, your women are all fictional and your men are actually historical and real." My first reaction was "Oh my God! What have I done here? Why have I done this?" And I said "I have to fix that. I have to introduce some historical women." And then I thought, "No, it's more interesting not to fix it, but to recognize it." And that's where the scene of Clytemnestra dreaming on the mountain at sunset comes in. Aeschylus, the writer (my position also) falls asleep for a moment and she gets a chance to create real women, historical figures. So she creates Isabella Duncan, Gertrude Stein and a whole series of women writers. And if we look at the history of writing and women, the place of women in writing, it's a male vision. Woman is a fictional creation of man. So how can a girl growing up, a girl becoming a woman...

LM: *...dream her way out of the fiction?*

RM: Yes, and become something else. It's very difficult. But, there's a crack, there's a crack there. And it occured to me, that in spite of me, my characters could resist my own fictionalizing of them. Or that I could at least indicate the problem, face it, deal with it, bring it out in some way.

LM: *I was reminded of Virginia Woolf's sense of how different it would be if historical women were able to live the strength, self-presence, public standing and grand exploits of the women who populate the pages of fiction.* City of Forgetting *explores the material lives of those inspiring women of fiction. In a sense, it locates them in history, places them on an historical stage* *alongside historical characters.*

RM: Yes, in a sense. It makes them physical, material. In this way they cannot become abstract, figures or symbols of something. That's part of it too.

LM: *Take a scene such as the tango on the Mountain which replays frag-ments of the stories of Clytemnestra and Lady Macbeth, particularly their relations to men. What's going on in that scene, in terms of the tango, in terms of the gender relations? What is the relation to the librarian, for example?*

RM: The librarian for me represents Marx. He first appears when his pocket is picked by Clytemnestra in the metro and she takes his library card. I mean, it's all she gets, unfortunately, and she keeps it. But he reappears as a case studied by Guevara when Guevara gets a job as an insurance agent on the lookout for people cheating on disabilities. Guevara's pretext for getting into the librarian's apartment is that he wants to interview him about negativity for an encyclopedia article. They sit down and get drunk together on vodka and rum. And then, as of that moment, little snippits of *Das Capital* slip into the old librarian's discourse. I never name him because he's like the father, the name of the Father or the God in the Jewish religion that you cannot pronounce. In the same way that in the Mohawk legend, the peace-maker Dekanaweda, founder of the Iroquois Confederation, is often referred to as "the one whose name must not be pronounced."

LM: *And by not naming him, he can play Agamemnon and other men with-in the scene; he can stand in for any of the them.*

RM: Exactly. He plays the father. And in my own experience, a huge part of the collapse of Marxism, had to do with issues of gender, with the inability of revolutionary movements to deal with women's issues on a practical level and to integrate feminism on a philosophical level. That failure then indicated a more profound or more general problem in Marxism: its totalizing vision. So I have this old librarian who is worn out, exhausted, barely able to get up, and incomprehensible. Ché desparately wants to find out straight from Marx's mouth what he said. (It's the old argument that if we can get back to the real Marx, find the true words of Marx, we can find the real socialism.) But, of course, Marx has had a stroke and he can't speak. We have access only to what Marx has become. And so Clytemnestra dances with the figure of Marx who becomes as they dance, the figure of Agamemnon, her husband, whom she is murdering. He is trying to reestablish his discourse, and she has her discourse: a great rage against Agamemnon who murdered her daughter and who instigated wars. At the same time you have Lady Macbeth experiencing her own murder of the king. They're all dancing on the Mountain to the tango which is Ché's favourite music. So for me it marks a crucial moment in the novel. It brings to a head all these conflicting discourses in a way that shows, to me anyway, how they clash and how they defeat themselves.

LM: *And it's happening in dance.*

RM: And it's happening in dance, yes. The tango is an interesting dance because it's a dance of machismo but it's also a dance of poor people and a dance coming out of the brothels. So it's a women's dance in many ways and even though it's a dance which rehearses the oppression of women, it can be subverted; it's full of contradictions, of conflict. The characters are dancing; they are celebrating; they are in a kind of unity. But at the same time they're playing out huge tensions that need to be played out in some way in order for us to understand and go on, go further.

LM: *The tango, like the opening scene of Clytemnestra on the Mountain, like the knife in the boot, they reminded me of Gail Scott's novels* Heroine *and* Main Brides. *How do these novels speak to each other?*

RM: Well, the tango as a matter of fact is a coincidence. I was working on that before Gail had finished *Main Brides*, before I had seen the novel. So that was an accident. The other two are very clearly references to Gail Scott's work. The most direct reference to *Heroine* is the black family up on the Mountain. Her book begins with a black man ...

LM: *... the tourist, the African-American tourist on the Mountain.*

RM: Yes. I found her whole dilemna about how to name him in the book really interesting. That reference was a way of acknowledging the existence of Montreal as a text in Gail Scott's work. I think her work is important for Montreal. And I think, for instance, that it would be foolish, even wrong, to write about Montreal in English without in some way writing from or about or through Gail Scott's Montreal. So I wanted to be able to dialogue with it in some way and to explore some of the things that she raises in her two novels. The knife in the boot was important to me because one of the things I found really positive about *Main Brides* was the way it ends with this young woman walking down the Main with a knife in her boot. To me, that's a symbol of resistance, of assertiveness and hope. But it was criticized for taking up male forms of violence, forms of resistance that are not womanly or something. I responded to this criticism in an an article I wrote about *Main Brides* a few years ago and I replayed it in the case of Suzy who is like that figure at the end of Gail's novel. So, it's always continuing. Gail says this and I say "Yes, and let's keep going with that figure. Let's not forget her." I like the idea of her moving from one book, from Gail's book, into my book.

LM: *But the name "Suzy Creamcheez" is new to your text, is it not?*

RM: No, she has roots in two places. One is Frank Zappa. He has a character in some of his songs called Suzy Creamcheez, which he invented. She's this California valley girl figure who floats mindlessly through his songs. But there's something about her that's interesting to me: this mindlessness, in some way, it resists. And then there's another movement which is Kathleen Martindale. Kathleen Martindale was a teacher and she was director of Women's Studies at York University for a while, and died a couple years ago now of cancer. She was a teacher of mine when I was in graduate school. I took a course with her and really learned a lot from her. I have enormous respect for her work and what she did. It was uncompromising and intelligent and gave a lot of thought to ethics. She wrote a piece, a fiction, not long before she died which had a character, really an autobiographical character, an academic called Suzy Creamcheez. It was a kind of hommage to Kathleen to take up that figure again. So Gail Scott was one and Kathleen was another woman who influenced my work. When I finished my first novel, people asked me where the women were. It was a very male novel and consciously so, because it was about undoing my maleness, about trying to analyze and understand what it meant to be a man at this time. For me, women were there in the novel but in many ways they had turned away from men; they had their own work to do and my job was to do my work. At the same time there is a danger that you can just turn away, you can do a Derrida in the sense of liquidating the problem of feminism. So women —women I know and figures of women — played a large part in the second novel. And that's how Suzy came to be, through that bizarre combination of different figures.

LM: *She's a central figure. She's the one who routinely forgets who she is; she's a girl who is also a boy. She has this way of repeating what other characters are saying and then stunning them into silence when she actually speaks; she's the one who closes the novel, who finds the library card*

Clytemnestra, a lover, has placed in her pocket and begins to explore the library. How do all these things come together? Who is Suzy Creamcheez?

RM: Well, they don't come together completely. I mean, I hope they don't come together. Suzy Creamcheez represents for me the impossibility of closure in the novel. Her echolalia is a form of resistance; it undermines other people's speech. At the same time, she's a figure with no memory. Her memory constantly dissolves and she has to reconstruct herself using anything around her including paper wrappers or a voice she hears in the street. And in so doing she sometimes constructs herself as a boy instead of as a girl. So gender slides. Sexuality slides. She's in love with Clytemnestra and sexually attracted to her. But there's no essentialism about Suzy, there's ...

LM: ... *no grand narrative.*

RM: There's no grand narrative possible because she doesn't know; she has no memory; she has never studied; she has never been in the library and she doesn't remember what she's learned. And yet she survives. She has a lot of strengths, a lot of skills. But she is also alone, unhappy, definitely not the glorified solution to the problem. And in the end, by putting her back in the library, I put the book back in the library where it comes from, where all the characters come from, where you can also go and find things that you need. The library for me is underground. To fight we need to study. People like Gail Scott, for instance, are intellectuals without being academics. They're not part of a system of knowledge and power, a system which killed Kathleen Martindale for me. But we still need to study and we need knowledge and we need the university in the ideal sense of the place. So I tried to bring Suzy there and see what would happen. I don't know what happens. For me it is a sign of hope. The whole city's been destroyed by an earthquake. All the characters are dead again. Suzy's alone, she's mourning, she's desperately running from the law, and she finds these books. But even at that moment of possibility in the library, she sees Pilote the dog chewing on something, probably the body of a human being. Signs of continuing terror alongside those of possibility. A figure of forgetting but also of resistance. All these things, to me, are what the book is about. And I just leave them there.

LM: *The library comes up in a variety of ways. Clytemnestra picks the pocket of the librarian and gets his library card. Just before he is killed, Le Corbusier tries to use the library card as I.D. Ché ends up working in the library with the librarian and literally drowns in a sea of discarded books.*

Suzy uses the card to get into the library at the end after the earthquake. What is happening to the library? Is it disintegrating?

RM: Yes, it is disintegrating. But even as it disintegrates as a system of codification, normalization, organization of disciplines and ideas into their proper categories, it opens up the possibility for recreating ways of knowing and thinking.

LM: *Because one can still read.*

RM: That's right. As long as one can get into the library. Suzy gets into the library when it's in ruins. The question is how to break down the library as system. The library card is a symbol of authority, of identity but it can also be a passage into something. Same for identity of the self: the question is how to break down the self without destroying the body and the person.

LM: *Right. Suzy, for instance, is constantly in the process of reconstructing herself. It's not that she needs a fixed sense of self but that she needs to go through the process.*

RM: Yes, she always has to reconstruct. And this is what the French writer Françoise Colin writes about the dilemma of post-structuralist feminism: the need to resist identity politics and essentialism when talking about women and at the same time the need to maintain the struggle for rights of women on a political level without some form of identity. You have to identify yourself ...

LM: *Yes, and it is difficult to speak if you don't have a position from which to speak. You have to have a sense of self.*

RM: Right. So, you construct on the barricades a shifting position and you build it long enough to speak, then you dismantle it quickly and move on and rebuild it. It's that kind of image of struggle that I am imagining and Suzy is that figure in a lot of ways because she's trying to do that. It's not easy to do. I don't know how to do it, but I long to find a way. And it's exhausting. It's difficult. It's painful at many moments. She pays an enormous price for it. But she has no choice because she hasn't been given any other options at this point.

LM: *I guess in a very immediate way, the library is also a warm place to go. Clytemnestra wants to secure a future for Suzy by providing her with that.*

RM: That's why she gives the library card to her, right? She originally kept it for that reason: in case things get tough in the winter, and you need a place to go to keep warm. Which is like the moment in my first novel when the prisoners in the concentration camp use the lime that's being poured over the dead bodies to warm themselves and even warm their food, to eat it. There is always this contradiction about the horror of what you're using to survive, but the necessity, in spite of that, to do it.

LM: *The second last chapter collages a myriad of scenes in which women characters kill themselves: Juliette, Ophelia, Cleopatra, Emma Bovary, Anna Karenina, Bertha Rochester, Lady Macbeth. What is that chapter about? What does* City of Forgetting *do with its difficult women?*

RM: Well it's the old idea about the novel, the nineteenth-century novel and much of the twentieth-century one, where women have two options: marriage or death. And often it's suicide or madness.

LM: *And in the case of a woman who's mad and disrupting the marriage plot — Bertha Rochester, for instance — she has to die too.*

RM: Yes. I wanted my characters to die in the novel. But there is a problem with killing off women in fiction. At the same time, I didn't want a positive image of the survival of these characters. So, once again, I had to find a way of making this dilemma visible. I did it through citations, references, intertextuality. And I did it in excess.

LM: *The scene gives the effect of one woman dying over and over again. It becomes overwhelming.*

RM: Yes, it's Lady Macbeth on the roof of the woman's shelter which has been surrounded by men and she's killing herself rather than be captured. That scene was a way of exploring the effect reading has. You said earlier "you can still read," but imagine the effect reading has when you're constantly killing yourself. It was also a way of exploring the problem of how as a male writer I could kill off women. Similarly, how can I write women having sex with each other. In that scene of grammatical and textual sex, I had to find some way of exploring that problem and making it visible too. So these are all tactics for me in writing, writing tactics to explore the problems of writing. That's all I really pretend to do in the novel: explore the problems.

LM: *What did the figure of Rudolf Valentino allow you to explore?*

RM: Valentino is interesting because he's a man who insists upon his hetero-sexuality but who takes great pleasure in dressing up. There is a kind of homosexuality to him that he denies but that is nevertheless there and that he is accused of. In fact, just before his death he was involved in a series of attacks and counter-attacks over his masculinity in the newspapers, where he challenged a writer to a boxing match to prove himself. But none of his marriages were consummated in spite of the fact that he married all these glamorous women. They all abandoned him when they found out he was a dud. At the same time he's silence. Working in silent film, he has no voice and in any case he doesn't speak their English well. He arrives as a poor immi-grant, Italian, landing in New York and he has to struggle enormously. He works as a dancer for hire in tea-houses.

LM: *In a sense, masculinity is already in question for him. Coming from Europe to the United States, he doesn't have a stable model.*

RM: That's right. He has to dance for money from women which is against his image of himself as the male who must protect the women and who cannot be bought by them or paid by them. He loves cross-dressing. If you look at his Sheik or his gaucho outfits, they're all forms of cross-dressing. There's a desire to be something else, to transgress but at the same time this fear of it. Valentino is interesting to me because he allows me, a heterosexual male author, to explore those elements of desire and fear within myself. He tries to negotiate his sexuality but he's unable to do it because of the context. And then his funeral: the response to his death was incredible; it turned into a riot.

LM: *When that response is transposed to the streets of Montreal, what happens?*

RM: It becomes gay pride day. I wanted to give Valentino back the possibility of gay pride.

LM: *Last question has to do with the dog.*

RM: Ah, the dog!

LM: *The representation of Pilote's interior monologue reminded me of Gertrude Stein's portraits. Some of her portraits attempted to get away from* *the tyranny of the noun and the proper name by dwelling in participles and impersonal pronouns. What's your sense of your strategy in portraying Pilote?*

RM: Stein was an influence, definitely. I wanted to get away from the subject. What interests me about the dog is that dogness does not have the same subjectivity as humanity; it does not have the same vision of the self. Pilote never says "I"; he doesn't say "he" or "you." He thinks of himself as an element in the pack or the group.

LM: *"This one" among several "other ones."*

RM: That's right. He calls himself "this one" and he thinks of "that one" or "the one that smells this way" or "tastes that way" or "looks so fierce."

LM: *Or "the first one" who is de Maisonneuve, founder of Montreal.*

RM: Yes, in the pack there is always a top dog and for him that's de Maisonneuve, who founded the city but who is also his master. I did a lot of reading about dogs, scientific reading, and I went to fiction to see how dogs are portrayed.

LM: *Most often they're personified.*

RM: They're personified; they're driven into humanness. I didn't want to do that. Dogs are often personified as stupid humans or childish humans because they're humans with less vocabulary. My dog has better vocabulary than the other characters. But it's only in one area: the sense of smell. He has a different perception of the self and of himself, and of his relationship to others. He also has this dog-eat-dog vision of the world. I mean, he doesn't have an ethics or any of the other crap humans are toying around with in the novel. And so, he does what he has to do to survive which includes swimming through the St. Lawrence river and eating other people if he has to. He has this indifference. Stein's dog, if you remember, says "thank you, thank you, thank you." She has a certain contempt for the dog because it is a domesticated animal. But Pilote to me is not entirely domesticated; he still has the wolf in him. And so, he's not a "thank you, thank you" dog. I was trying to get a character in the novel that wasn't human at all. Suzy is not human in many ways, or in humanist ways but the dog is even less so. But again, how can I as a human pretend to be a dog? I don't pretend to be Pilote just as I don't claim to be Clytemnestra. I claim only that I am exploring the problem of writing and reading Pilote, exploring the problem of the other, of the other as a writer. And of how to remain open to the other without appropriating the other. That's the insoluble problem of writing which keeps you writing.

Lianne Moyes teaches in Études anglaises *at l'Université de Montréal. This interview appeared in* Matrix #52.

Marie-Claire Blais

Interviewed by **ELAINE KALMAN NAVES**

ELAINE KALMAN NAVES: *Where is home for you now?*

MARIE-CLAIRE BLAIS: Well, I live mostly in the Eastern Townships. And also I'm in Key West. Since the 1960s I'm in and out of the States a lot. In the 60s, when I received a Guggenheim Fellowship, I went to live in Cambridge, Mass. — so it has stayed with me to go back and forth. Maybe I have an abnormal nature.

EN: *There's a lot of freedom in that.*

M-CB: But it's very nerve-wracking to go around the world the whole time — because I do a lot of readings.

EN: *Your most recent title is a collection of short stories.*

M-CB: Yes, that appeared at the end of 1992.

EN: *The short story form is a departure for you, isn't it?*

M-CB: I wrote a few before, but in magazines. I published them in a European magazine called *Atelier imaginaire*.

EN: *One of the things that interests me is that when someone becomes famous, all these legends start to proliferate. So one of the sources says that you began to write when you were six [laughter], another that you were nine, and a third that you were eleven.*

M-CB: It was closer to eleven. But it was all the time in my head.

EN: *You knew you were going to do this.*

M-CB: Yes.

EN: *And you knew that you were going to do this in a situation where it was not at all common to write.*

M-CB: I felt that I was driven to do so. I knew that it would be my life very young.

EN: *Somewhere, in an autobiographical essay, you've written, "Life is unbearable without the solace of writing."*

M-CB: I must have gotten it from a book or something [laughter]. I love life very much, very much! But, well, I could not imagine my life without writing. You're more relaxed certainly if you're not a writer.

EN: *Especially the approach that you take to your writing. You're very rigorous with your research and in what you impose upon yourself. You live your characters, is that not so?*

M-CB: And also everyone else when I look around me.

EN: *You live everyone else around you?*

M-CB: I look at them: it's part of me, it's part of them. At some point, when you write a book, they become you. Then you become kind of objective and detached. Until you get into another book. Then you get upset again.

EN: *It upsets you because it is working in you or because of what you're seeing?*

M-CB: It's also because it is very demanding. The time you're writing the book, all the characters become very demanding. You would prefer to just enjoy yourself — but you can't. This can last for six months or for two years.

EN: *The project swallows you.*

M-CB: Yes you're in it for a long time.

EN: *Another one of these legends that I read was that* La Belle Bête *took you fifteen days to write.*

M-CB: That *was* true. But it's a very imperfect book [laughing]. I will never do that again. I was very young then. Now I take so much time to write in the sense that I don't have that kind of spontaneity anymore. Now I have more control. But at that time I could not control it.

EN: *You're more conscious of what you're doing.*

M-CB: Yes.

EN: *And at that time it just had to come out.*

M-CB: Yes, the first one did. It was like a tale.

EN: *I was speaking to the poet Louis Dudek a few days ago, and he said that when he writes poetry, he knows right away. It's something that he receives. It's just there. And he's almost just a medium for it.*

M-CB: Yes. That's beautiful. He's right. It's in the receiving.

EN: *He's a very rational, non-religious kind of person, but he said it's almost a holy thing. You, too, have said something like that. You've made a distinction between some of your works which you call "critical books," where you deal with controversial issues, and "sacred books," which are more organic.*

M-CB: Yes. For sure there are some works that are more difficult and more luminous.

EN: *Is it the sacred ones that are more difficult?*

M-CB: Yes. I think the most difficult writing — your poet friend is very right — that is what takes time …. The refinement is a long process.

EN: *Because you don't know how much to tamper with, how much you're interfering with the original core …. As a child, you won a scholarship to the convent Saint-Roch du Québec?*

M-CB: Yes. That was a very long time ago. But even though I did, I was never a very good student.

EN: *But you read a great deal. You managed in secret to get your hands on great books.*

M-CB: I met a few teachers who helped me. It was classical studies, so the teachers had to be good.

EN: *What were some of the books that influenced your imagination?*

M-CB: These days, when you're in school, you learn a lot about the poetry of Emile Nelligan and Saint-Denys Garneau. But then, by myself, I read Malraux. It's strange to me now that I was mostly interested in the works of men. I discovered women writers much later.

EN: You were reading Malraux when you were a young teen?

M-CB: I loved all these books written by Camus and Malraux. They were on our reading list. I'm not sorry — it was great learning. But I became attached to women's writing much later, when I was sixteen.

EN: *I think I read somewhere that you wrote imitation novels based on the Brontes.*

M-CB: Between the ages of twelve and fourteen I wrote a lot. But it was all imitation, I threw it all away except for a few poems.

EN: *I want to get a little bit of sense from you of that time in Québec. It was a closed time because of the Church —*

M-CB: Yes. But it was worse for people who came before. In my teens — all the girls in my convent were absolutely against the Church. Everything was breaking down. And the nuns had terrible difficulties making sure we'd be good, be obedient, keep our faith. We were already in a state of revolt. It was already over.

EN: *Something had already changed?*

M-CB: Yes. One cannot say it was the same for the people who came ten years before. They had many more problems.

EN: *But still you did want to get away.*

M-CB: Yes, I was attracted to the idea of going away.

EN: *You came first to Montreal.*

M-CB: I did all kinds of little jobs. Like many young people then, I had a very hard time — working and trying to write. But I was saved by writing. Because writing novels — I was helped by that.

EN: *In your own self, you mean?*

M-CB: Yes. And when I began to write poetry, I was helped, too. Writing was always like an angel over my head. It gave me faith.

EN: *I see the image of you from that autobiographical essay that you wrote when you were very young and you were at home and there were your younger brothers and sisters — and you wanted to have your own place. In the end, your parents helped you get one — although they thought there was no future in what you wanted to do.*

M-CB: [Laughing] They were good parents. I was lucky in that. They are very good and I received a very good education. But, naturally, the life of a writer is something that takes on its own life. But thank God I was in a very good family.

EN: *So* The Manuscript of Pauline Archange *was not entirely autobiographical.*

M-CB: No, no! It was taken from people I saw in the lower classes, people I saw as a child who were much poorer.

EN: *When I hear your story, it reminds me a little bit of Jovette Marchessault's, too, in the sense of this incredible need to write — and without the encouragement in the immediate surroundings to do something with it. And yet it would come out. With her it came out much later in her life than with you.*

M-CB: But it came out! Jovette has been very very courageous about that novel. She wrote it very well. The light at the end .... When she became free to write, she was saved.

EN: *There's also that scene in your little essay when you meet Edmund Wilson at the Ritz-Carlton in Montreal. I thought that was so charming. They wouldn't serve you a drink because they thought you were under age.*

M-CB: I was very young. And he was so impressive. And so was his wife [Elena] who arranged it all. I guess I felt a great sense of [their] age. [Laughing]. And there *was* [a big disparity in age]. And of education and everything. For me they seemed more European than American —

EN: *He recognized a great talent in you.*

M-CB: It was wonderful. Even that first day, he began to speak to me about a new life. He said, "You will meet many writers in Cambridge." He began to give me a sense of a new life .... But I already had one. Because I'd already spent a year in Paris.

EN: *And published, I think, three books by that time.*

M-CB: Yes.

EN: *He was recognizing someone with talent and some achievement.*

M-CB: Yes — but he might not have done. Because he was not inclined to love women's literature. A *few* went under his compassionate look — he loved Edna St. Vincent Millay, Virginia Woolf (although not completely), the Bronte sisters — but I don't remember him feeling about women writers the way his wife felt.

EN: *You think she influenced him?*

M-CB: Yes. He was always full of doubts about what a woman could do. [Laughing] That was the time! But it was amazing that despite his lack of vision — in spite of himself — he could see someone like Edna St. Vincent Millay, that he recognized Mary McCarthy as a great talent. But I think *she* was so strong, she could show it. He loved strong women.

EN: *The power and influence a critic like that could have, when they have these prejudices ....*

M-CB: He could be with you for one or two of your books, but with other works he could not understand at all. Just because your vision was not his own. He could be very unfair. Like with Bernanos. He could not recognize his great strength .... But we are all imperfect, and as you say, too much power.

EN: *In the beginning, here in Québec, critics did not understand your work.*

M-CB: In the beginning I had a hard time.

EN: *Did that hurt a lot?*

M-CB: That was typical. Yes. It was not my milieu. The people who were rough on me were the same ones who were rough on Michel Tremblay. The university people. People who thought that writing should go through universities.

EN: *But at the same time* La Belle Bête *went through two editions very quickly.*

M-CB: Yes. It was translated into English and it was published in France.

EN: *But it received an immediate recognition locally, too.*

M-CB: Well, yes, after the international recognition, it comes back here. And it was a bit like that with *A Season In The Life Of Emmanuel.*

EN: *Are you working on something now?*

M-CB: I'm working on a book set in Key West. It's mostly about the U.S.A., but for you when you read it, it will not seem very American [laughing] — it will not seem like anything but that's probably because I'm turning it into something of my own.

EN: *Is it dark?*

M-CB: I don't think so .... Because there's the sea, there is the air.

EN: *When we read you, though, we see the darkness. I'm talking, I guess, about* Anna's World *or* Pierre — *where we witness these very apocalyptic scenes. It's a very scary — and very true — view of the world. But you will say, there is light, a character is viewed through sunshine, for instance. But at the heart of things for you, isn't there a lot of darkness?*

M-CB: No. I think I have a joyful character.

EN: Yourself, yes, I can see that.

M-CB: I love life, and, if I listened to myself, I would go out all the time and have fun with my friends. I have to impose on my joyful nature a much harder view which I still don't have.

EN: *It's not natural for you?*

M-CB: It's not natural, even in the practice of writing. Sometimes I really forget that you have to be absolutely straight and rigorous. You know you could forget it, if you have a good temperament for laughing. I don't feel dark. I describe my vision of the world, but the souls of the people, for example, in the case of *Visions d'Anna*, it is Anna — our generation — who is apocalyptic. Because she's almost a child of the year 2000. Well, *Anna* was written a long time ago, but in the book she could be a child of the year 2000.

It is a book about our own time — our actual time, the way we live, the way we hurt our resources, the way we destroy everything for the youth of today. So it is apocalyptic in that sense — I think it is a *vision* of something, seen by someone who is young among adults.

And also like another book, *Deaf To The City*. That is maybe my darkest book, but it is a book not only about suicidal feelings but also about redemption: through love that doesn't come. Love doesn't come, but it is there in the book all the time. Florence is constantly loving people but cannot feel anything. That's a study of what it is to be in the kind of terrible situation that I call desperation.

EN: *Is* Deaf To The City *still your favourite among your books?*

M-CB: [Laughing] Well, maybe my favourite will be the next one. I hope so. With all the demands.

EN: *I hear you say, "If I listen to myself, I am joyful. I have a zest for living, I love to go out with my friends," ... but when you write, you're also listening to yourself, aren't you?*

M-CB: Yes, Yes. I put myself in a difficult situation though. I go to the country. But I don't like to live in the country. I put myself in an austere place so I won't be —

EN: *Distracted? And then what comes to you there, that's a vision?*

M-CB: Yes. I get something for this austerity. I would prefer to be in Key West [laughing]. But in Key West, I just close my door, too, the same way as I do in the country.

EN: *Do you live by yourself in Key West?*

M-CB: I have a little room in Key West. It's not a possession, it's a rented room. But I close it, the way I close my room in the country. The only thing is, it's more cheerful because I see writers all the time who are in the same situation as I am, who are working from morning 'til night and going out at night. I see wonderful writers who are older and give me courage.

EN: *So you're working there, too.*

M-CB: Oh, I'm writing all the time.

EN: *Are you using a word processor yet?*

M-CB: Not yet! After this book. I work on typewriters but they're always breaking. So I'm resigned to a word processor. I will like it, I think.

EN: *There's a wonderful thing you said once. "What tortures me is the fragility of people, how fragile they are, how easily they crumble."*

M-CB: Yes. Sensitive people are generally frail inside.

EN: *And yourself?*

M-CB: I have a lot of strength, I think, in spite of everything.

EN: *It must take a lot of strength to enter these lives and to face these visions: to imagine oneself into the year 2000 or to go and see the motorcycle people.*

M-CB: That is also in the year 2000, but that's very close by now.

EN: *When you wrote it years ago, people said what you described was too extreme.*

M-CB: The things I wrote about in *Anna's World*, they happen, but if we write about them, it's to prevent them, not for them to happen. It's the writer's work. It's the writer's work to see a little bit down the road.

EN: *Do you think there's hope for our world?*

M-CB: Probably. If we want it. There's a little more in the past few years — I think we're more conscious of what we're losing. So there's a rebellion against losing everything, against losing the Earth, losing the next generation of people.

EN: *Mary Meigs has written a lot about her relationship with you. Do you feel comfortable if I mention in my article that you had a long-standing relationship with her?*

M-CB: Yes, you could say that.

EN: *Are you no longer friends?*

M-CB: Oh, yes we are. Maybe it's a delicate subject. But she's a great, great friend. We see each other all the time now. I admire her very much. She's a great woman. It is in her house that I work in the country, when she herself is not there. I saw her in Key West and I will be seeing her at a conference she will be attending shortly in Hamilton.

EN: *You've written that the solitude of a woman is unique.*

M-CB: Yes, and that will come back again in the book I'm writing now. Mary also explained that much, much better. It's hard for a woman to be an artist, and it is hard for her to do the same things as men do. It's also hard to be a woman. There is solitude.

EN: *Is it hard to do the things that men do because we have things to do? Or is it hard to do the things that men do because they're not for us?*

M-CB: The justice is not established yet. It is coming through but slowly. But we see that other people don't see how important the feminist movement is. When women try to do things, it's cold. This revolution belongs to us. It was born a long time ago when women won the vote, but actually it was latent a long time even before. Still, we're reproached for going too fast. That's part of Mary's writing that I find very important. In her autobiography [*Lily Briscoe: A Self-Portrait*] she describes the hardships she went through trying to be a woman artist — to choose celibacy. A man would have done that then without question.

EN: *So that when you talk of women's solitude, you're talking of artistic solitude?*

M-CB: But also yours — a woman trying to speak to her daughters, the evolution of daughters in this society.

In the book I'm writing now, I'm coming back to these characters like Florence—who don't know what they want but want to break the chain of conventional unity which is man/woman/family .... They don't necessarily want to join any particular kind of orientation — they want a breakthrough, a vision. What Emily Dickinson was trying to find. And this is something for each woman to decide. A man, too, but a man is very busy with his own egocentricity in the world. In the sense that he's participating in *anything* in the world: he's in politics, in science, he's everywhere.

Now we could have women everywhere, but it's just so difficult to do!

EN: *I'm often made uncomfortable by the emphasis on the vulnerability of women. Of course, it's there. But I see so many men who are at a loss these days, who don't know what's expected of them these days.*

M-CB: They're trying to find their places. My feelings are not at all fanatical. I understand much of what's happening in men's consciousness and in the pressure felt by male artists and writers.

The same doubt, the same anguish, very close.

This interview was conducted in the offices of the Goodwin Literary Agency, as research for Elaine Kalman Naves' collection of essays, The Writers of Montreal *(Véhicule Press, 1993). The interview appeared in* Matrix *#43.*

David Fennario

Interviewed by **Terence Byrnes**

Terence Byrnes: Place Ville Marie, *your new, 'fictionalized' autobiography, will be published this winter. Why are you writing prose rather that plays now?*

David Fennario: I can't think of a single play I've done that I'm satisfied with.

I found that a couple of plays I attempted to do six or seven years ago could easily be prose and would probably work better as prose. That's when I realized that my style was changing ... and I wasn't quite sure I could make my ideas work dramatically. I've been rereading a lot of theatrical work and taking time off before I move on.

Also, I'm just not getting the productions. My relationship with the Centaur has been uncomfortable for quite a few years and I'm not directly linked into any other theatre group. At a time of cutbacks in the arts, the theatre scene is suffering. I'm even thinking of writing poetry again for the first time in maybe about 25 years.

TB: *In* Fennario, *a recent NFB film that chronicles your troubled relationship with the Centaur Theatre, you and Maurice Podbrey look awfully uneasy with each other.*

DF: What a moment. What a moment.

TB: *Podbrey says, at one point, that the Centaur is where you learned your stagecraft and you answer, quite tersely, "No I didn't." Where did you acquire your skills, if not from your apprenticeship with the Centaur?*

DF: Podbrey had read my book, *Without a Parachute*, and gave me the chance to sit in on two seasons of Centaur rehearsals. I wasn't particularly interested in theatre but it meant a grant and an opportunity. I was very prompt — it was almost like I was punching a time card — and I didn't speak much to the actors or the directors and I had no real sort of judgment of what was happening. I was waiting for the secret of what acting is — or of what directing is — to be revealed to me. I think I understood more than I realized.

A lot of the stuff I saw was just real crap. Actually it was the worst of those plays, *Autumn at Altenburg*, that inspired me and gave me the courage to attempt to write *On the Job*. My first plays are very much like films because I learned so little sitting in on those rehearsals.

My first play, *On the Job*, was a fucking monster hit — so there wasn't encouragement for me to go through a learning process. You got a hit, you must know what you're doing, right? But I think that delayed the actual craft, the skill I now have as a playwright. At the same time I think that *On the Job*, *Nothing to Lose*, and *Balconville* all contain scenes as good as anything I've seen on the Canadian stage.

Success is distancing. It's alienating. It's elitist. It wasn't something I particularly planned for. I think that's important to understand. I didn't plan to do that.

TB: *So you were writing with your native, but untutored talent?*

DF: Um-hm. Also, I lucked into Guy Sprung, who directed my plays at Centaur. He was really good help in the earlier drafts, telling me what could work dramatically. These conversations with him would be maybe ten minutes long. But it's enough ... if it makes sense to you, and if you have an ear. Even if you don't understand the dramatic form as well as you could.

TB: *Were you the kind of naturally theatrical kid who made others laugh with his mimicry?*

DF: Nothing to compare to some of the guys I grew up with. But it was an art form where I grew up — storytelling and showing it.

In my generation — we had at least eight years before television became a big deal — you really would express yourself through telling the story with gestures. I've been complimented by actors on that, although I don't consider myself really good at it.

TB: *Do you think this kind of storytelling was more common on "the Avenues" where you grew up in Verdun that it was elsewhere?*

DF: I'm pretty sure it's a working class phenomenon in general, but where I grew up there was an Irish flavour to it and they're masters.

TB: *Did you have a family storyteller?*

DF: My mother. I think it helps if you only go to grade two, which was her case.

As I got older I realized the very bottom tone of all my writing is the tone my mother used in storytelling. I mean the best of my stuff. So she's actually a main influence — or perhaps the 'big ear' that they say I have for the way people speak.

I still carry what I had from my community — where your whole idea of status and prestige was sports — and from my mother, so I never quite became comfortable with the written word. That primary training I had stuck with me. And I don't see it all as negative — from a class sense, you know.

TB: *For you, is there any distinction between art or craft and politics?*

DF: One of the main politicizing things in my life was my determination to become an artist, coming up against barriers and being told, "You can't be..." and continuing to try.

If you grow up in an environment like Verdun, you don't really come across the middle class — except for the landlord and except for the principal in the school and some of the teachers. So you don't actually have sense of a class society ... especially when I was young. This area was such a ghetto. You're stuck between the Lachine Canal, two sets of railways and you went uptown twice a year, to the St. Patrick's day Parade and the Santa Claus parade, and that was it.

I remember the I.Q. test they had in school and I wasn't among the elite four or five kids who did well and were being treated differently from the rest — and they *were* treated differently. The rest of us were told just to be quiet and sit there. If you're inclined to be able to think quite linear and quite middle class you're going to score better than some other kid.

TB: *You equate a kind of reasoning or logic with class?*

DF: I think so.

Just going to school was terrible. I mean, to go off the streets where we were all playing and doing our number and all of a sudden you're shoved in this prison. It was like Duplessis Québec prison ....

By some fluke I was in a class that was a mixture of Latin [college-bound] and Science and I was called to see the guidance teacher with the class. He literally pointed to McGill University through the window, saying, "This is the place you're going to go. You are the chosen." I got all excited 'cause I'd never had a teacher talk to me that way before. So I went up to him and he asked me, "What are you interested in?" and I said "Writing," and he said, "What kind of writing?" "Just writing in general, I want to be a writer." And he said, "What's your name again?" I think he spotted the fact that I had my sleeves rolled up, which was a sign your were in Science, and he said, "You're in Science 2. What are you doing here? Get back to class."

And the following week they told Science 2, "Here are the brochures we have on being an electrician, on driving a truck."

TB: *In* Place Ville Marie, *you say that anyone chained to a factory life might become a serial killer or a revolutionary. Do you feel that self is defined totally by work or the conditions of work?*

DF: Class defines people more than anything else. And class would define what kind of work you do and the work you do certainly influences a large part of your life, particularly if you feel that this is your life forever. And that can make you quite angry, quite bitter, and can turn you into a very nasty personage. A lot of the serial killers that they've caught in the States are very conservative in their politics.

TB: *Gary, a character in* On the Job, *says, "Sometimes I wish everything I hate in life had just one face." Does everything that you hate have the face of class division?*

DF: In theory, we have a democracy. You can vote for anyone you want — at least in theory. But we have no democracy at work. If you're lucky, you have a union to defend you, but we don't control the hospitals, even though we work in them. We don't control the schools. We don't control how cars are made. That's controlled by a very small percentage of people and by the bureaucracy they appoint and/or the politicians that they control. We should be able to vote in our own management and determine how things are manufactured, how the schools are run, and how the hospitals are run.

There's another book that I'm working on — my working title's *Glory Days* — about my early days in the theatre. My sudden ascent into the whole milieu was at a time when I wasn't politically prepared for it. For example, some of the humour in *On the Job* was quite racist, which titillated the middle class audience in a way that I perhaps didn't mean. At the same time, [the play] could be constructed as being anti-union. I was seeing it as a critique from the left.

TB: *The audience saw your treatment of some of these working-class* *characters as comic?*

DF: It happened — that was, at times. Audience is about 50% of a play, especially a new play. The audience will pull it a certain direction ... and it pulled me, I think, because I didn't have the political understanding that I later developed. I don't think it's any coincidence that so many working-class artists are fucked up over success because you're groomed for failure. You can handle failure, you can handle fuck-ups, but success is something that you're not prepared for.

I found myself thinking along the lines of, "Yeah, I probably deserved this success. I mean, you know, here I am." And you start thinking, "Yeah, you know, these [middle-class] people are cool. They're human, you know. They're intelligent; they're sensitive." All of that's true, but it doesn't make a difference in an historic sense, in a concrete sense, in a social sense. I was in the process of sleeping with the enemy.

In all my interviews I identified myself as a Marxist, as a socialist, but I really wasn't applying it. You can get away with saying you're a Marxist or that you're a revolutionary if you're not doing anything about it.

TB: *Isn't a good playwright a member of an elite?*

DF: Theatre isn't just a playwright sitting with his book. You're dealing with actors, you're dealing with a director, you're dealing with someone doing the sound, doing the lights. You're dealing with a live audience. It's immediate. In theatre, if you're working mainstream, you're also dealing with class on a real basis because, right off the top, you're doing auditions. Which means there's two or three people behind the table buying the other people, the actors, who come to show their wares. If there's any proletariat in theatre, it's actors.

TB: *Aren't you being evasive? Isn't anyone who is driven by those needs to produce a superior work also a person who is, in some ways, stepping outside a community of equality?*

DF: In this society you either compromise with the middle class or you don't get work.

What I think I haven't compromised on — at least consciously — has been what I write. There's been a lot of times, especially to get a show done, that I've had to keep my mouth shut or kiss ass. But the writing is what I want to say.

As for the big question about whether I sold out or not ... I've been trying to sell out for 25 years. [laughter] But there's not too many Marxist-Leninists that they want to buy. I've been trying my best. I just fucked it up.

TB: *At the end of* Balconville, *the unemployed burned-out and generally miserable characters turn to the audience and say, "What are we going to do?" Why are they asking a middle-class, theatre-going audience for guidance?*

DF: No, it's not a good ending for the Centaur. I had two endings and I think I should have stuck with the first, where they talk amongst the furniture [thrown on the street to save it from a fire] and it just sort of fades out. You get the general impression that they've learnt a lesson. Whereas I went through the agitational thing, which doesn't work at the Centaur. So if the Centaur does it again, we'll go back to the other ending.

TB: *You must know that when Premier Bouchard spoke to the anglo audience at the Centaur last fall, he referred to your plays.*

DF: I was there. The invited elite.

TB: *An economically mainstream party citing you as a source of inspiration for anglophones is laden with ironies.*

DF: Yeah. I have a pretty good guess that I'm on the outs with any anlgophone group that I can think of in Québec at this point because I've become quite outspoken in Québec's right to self-determination. Yeah. I voted "Yes" in 1980 and "Yes" in '95.

TB: *A Pequiste "Yes"?*

DF: No. Definitely not. That's why I don't have a steady job. I mean if I played it smart I would have kissed their ass, but I can't because Bouchard's racist. So is Parizeau. I voted "Oui" because it was a vote for change, a vote for the right to negotiate, and it was a vote against cutbacks. I don't see separation as a solution by any means, but at the same time I support Quebec's right to self-determination just like I do with the Cree and the Mohawk.

TB: *In your introduction to your prose collection* Blue Mondays, *you yearn for a Québec that "Lets us love ... Won't turn us sour ... Doesn't kill its poets." Do you think that a separate Québec would be like that?*

DF: That same thing can apply to whether Québec stays in Canada or not. I think at a period when the unions in Québec are so influenced by nationalism that they're allowing Bouchard to sharpen his knife in terms of cutbacks to social services that it would be quite a disaster for the workers ... for Québec to separate. At the same time, Québec is being driven to it, as far as I'm concerned, because of the attacks from the Reform Party, by Chrétien, by the insistence that Québec doesn't even get recognition as a distinct society, it's driving Québec toward separation. It's driving Québec into the arms of Bouchard, who'll make Mike Harris look like a sweetheart if he has his chance. So it would be a disaster for the workers.

TB: *How did you become an actor as well as a playwright?*

DF: *Banana Boots* is the only show I've done as performer on a constant level. But a lot of my readings have become performances by now.

A high percentage of actors and dancers come from working-class backgrounds. These are physical art forms. It's the emphasis you grew up with. I have a good friend from Verdun who was, for two years, a champion in gymnastics in Québec. He went on to become a doctor of sports psychology and he told me how the Russians found their gymnasts. They'd go around to all the schools in the working-class areas and find the kids who were hopping around like crazy and they'd pull them out and say, "You're going to be a gymnast." I think theatre schools should do the same thing. Go around to all these working-class schoolyards, look at the guys who are acting up and give them the training.

Something I've noticed in auditions is that you'll get a larger percentage of actors who come from a middle-class background. Unfortunately, I would say a large percentage of them have a carrot up their ass-holes because it's put there by their training, by their grooming: You gotta sit up straight. You gotta eat right. You gotta talk right. You gotta think right. So it stiffens you up and you don't have the physical looseness that an actor needs. It's a handicap, I think, to be middle class. It doesn't mean you can't have a Sir Laurence Olivier; it doesn't mean you can't have middle-class actors who are as good as any you'll ever see, but it's a class handicap.

TB: *The presence of Liz, your wife, haunts your autobiographical books —*

DF: My *partner*. Liz. Yeah.

TB: *Yet the life that's portrayed in your plays is usually the life of work and the street. Why isn't that part of your life represented by your mother, by*

Liz, by your own kids, in your theatre?

DF: I did try to put some of my family situation in *Moving*. Unfortunately, it was a failed piece. One of the stipulations that I have with Liz is that we keep that stuff private 'cause so much else of me has been so public.

We've been together for so long. And is has been the combination of being lovers and comrades. I don't think it would have lasted if we hadn't become comrades, and the relationship become politicized. A relationship that doesn't get politicized tends to be reactionary. If you're not moving forward, if you're not fighting against women's oppression —

TB: *Isn't there some level of life or intimacy that doesn't exclude politics, but exists in addition to it?*

DF: I think if people aren't looking outward at the real causes of some of their reactions to each other, the larger causes, then they tend to blame each other. They tend to victimize each other, to see [the cause] as their own private problem, their own personal fault, whereas the situation they're in is largely determined by the social situation that we live in — especially poverty. You know the expression, "Poverty walks in the door, love goes out the window."

I wouldn't say there's a helluva lot of love and care on the Avenues.

TB: *Was there love in your family?*

DF: I can't remember being hugged by my mother. I'm sure when I was young it happened. I know a lot of middle-class people are going to shrinks for the same thing, but I grew up and it was the norm.

The positive side of this was it was part of a reality which you're going to have to face in your life, and also a solidarity in the sense of "nobody's better than anybody else." Nobody had any pretensions ... and the walls are thin anyhow. You can hear everything.

I understand gang mentality because the kids would gang up together; we would seek it from each other 'cause we each had big families in those days, too. So your mother was popping out another kid and you're out on the street ... [the lack of attention] wasn't somebody's particular characteristic fault. It was a social thing of poverty, of tension, of being treated like shit on the job and coming home.

TB: *The egalitarianism of "We're all the same" sounds like it's tinged with another feeling: "We're all the same because we're all shit." And if fault is* *never "somebody's particular characteristic fault," you can't take responsibility for your own individuality.*

DF: But some of these memories are so concrete! What we had in the 50s was the beginnings of a fight back, the beginnings of being unionized. What did that mean, getting unionized? It meant you got better pay and you got better hours. And it meant you didn't have to wait until your arm was fuckin' pulled off. It meant that maybe you got two weeks vacation so you could take a break and do something with the kids and wife besides yelling. Things the middle class would take for granted or would be bored with or say there's bigger problems than this, or shit like that.

But if you just have poverty, anxiety, insecurity ... You put any animal in that situation and they don't behave well. Especially if they don't think they can escape it. Then they turn on each other. That's why their politics are very important. Because if you're working class there's only one way out of it and that's organizing and solidarity. Not individuals. The individual, elitist thing of the middle class.

TB: *Have you written anything set more recently than 1980? Are you starting to feel constrained by the fact that you're no longer living in a world that resembles the one you're writing about?*

DF: I haven't really thought of that question.

TB: *I'm afraid that someone's going to come along one of these days and say, "David Fennario, I remember him — the Lech Walesa of Canadian theatre. He came from the working class and he galvanized us all for a while and he was at the top and now he's back in the shipyard, invisible."*

DF: And I'll say, "Go fuck yourself 'cause I've had a good life. If I die now I had a good fuckin' life, so go fuck yourself!"

Terence Byrnes, then a Matrix *editor and photographer, interviewed David Fennario in Verdun (where they both live) for* Matrix #48.

Nick Bantock

Interviewed by **ANDY BROWN**

NICK BANTOCK: *There Was An Old Lady* was my first pop-up book, the first thing I ever did. I was working with this guy who did pop-up books and I realized that he had all this success but couldn't even draw. I can draw, what's stopping me? Then a little light came on and I went home and came up with this idea, took about three or four days to put it together, sent it off and they accepted it. There was no battle to get published.

ANDY BROWN: *How did you manage the mechanics of this?*

NB: I sat down with cardboard and masking tape and got other people's pop-up books and ripped them apart, to see how it worked. I started off simple. You can't be much simpler than this: it's a cut, a fold, and another fold sticking through. Then it started to get a bit more complicated. So you can see my learning process quite literally. In fact with *Wings* I got much more adventurous. Here's a dragonfly and you can move the wings back and forth. This is the Japanese version of the book. You can't get this anywhere now.

AB: *Do these sell well in Japan?*

NB: Yeah. This book had a total print run of 70,000. For a pop-up book that's quite a lot.

AB: *Does all your time go into these books? Are you able to make a living at this?*

NB: Well, with the pop-ups it's pathetic. You get 1% on nothing. When I did *Griffin and Sabine* it was enough to set me up. Unfortunately taxes take 30% and a seperation and divorce takes another 50%, so basically I've watched it dwindle away. But that's okay. The doors are still open and what counts is not the money but the power to have someone back your ideas, not having to spend six months going around with your cap in your hand. I did a CD ROM called *Ceremony of Innocence*, into which Peter Gabriel's company Real World invested $1 million. It won every major international award it possibly could but didn't even get a line in ordinary newspapers, and didn't sell. But I can call up a big publishing house in New York and be taken seriously and that is worth its weight in gold.

AB: *I notice that you are moving from very interactive books, like pop-ups or* Griffin and Sabine, *which had pockets and envelopes, to something like the recent* The Museum at Purgatory *where text and image are not as integrated.*

NB: Originally the books were more structually integrated. But with [*Museum*] I tried to integrate thematically, so that the image is very much part of the narrative. This is fresh ground. I don't have anyone to look to and see how to do it, to learn from. I feel like it's a very slow process in establishing, essentially, a new genre. I wish there were more people working in it .... If I could look to other people and ask them how they are solving these problems it would be easier, but there is next to nothing out there. In the mainstream of the West there is a polarization, where you have to choose one thing or the other. There is a discomfort with middle ground. Just look at the way publishing houses are set up, they're very specialized. You have reviewers who only do literary stuff. It's often very hard for a newspaper to find someone who is actually capable of reviewing these things, someone who is comfortable in words and images. You can read reviews constantly where they've understood the text but the images are just pretty pictures. That's all they get. Yes, Griffin is lonely and looking for a lover, but that is where most reviewers stop. There are all these other levels, like visual jokes or alchemical references ....

Humour is another way you can allow people to go deeper. We have stylized religion, we have dogma, we have individual thought but we've somehow gotten to the point where we say that the philosophers have done all that before, so we'll just go watch television. But to me life is about curiosity and asking questions. When I give readings I say that I haven't got a single answer but I'm very good at asking questions. If you are a skeptic you believe anything is possible. If you want to discover something about an object you can cast a shadow. Then if you circumnavigate the object with the light you still haven't seen the object but you have an understanding of its shape. It's like a bat sending out radar signals and seeing how long it takes them to bounce back. I feel I have been extremely lucky stumbling on an arena where I can talk about these things, have some fun, and get paid. It's a privileged position but like all privileges you have to make use of it. There's a responsibility to other people who want to do the same thing. You need to be the pointy edge of the wedge.... I think that five or six years down the road we are going to see a whole slew of this kind of stuff.

AB: *I hope so.*

NB: Instead of publishers saying, "This is an interesting possibility, let's do more," they say, "Oh, this is a one-off. It's a freak. We'll just carry on doing what we've always done." But they're missing the point.

AB: *One thing I wanted to talk to you about was stamp design. I know you are a serious collector. What's interesting to me about stamps is that they're a functional combination of words and images. You've designed stamps, but not for real countries, which seems more interesting.*

NB: That way you don't get any of the aggravation. Barb [Barbara Hodgson and Bantock form the design company Byzantium] has done stamps for Canada Post, but I wouldn't want to be involved in that because they're so petty and pedantic in their attitudes. I got interested in the whole area of stamps totally by accident. I was doing a book cover, because that's what I used to do, and it was a book about Spain in 1945. I wanted an image that would pinpoint that place and time and I thought that the best thing to do would be to try and find a stamp. I went to a place called The Corn Market, a little stamp store in Bristol. I got to chatting with the clerk and the conversation was really interesting. So I found myself going down there every morning and just hanging around listening to his conversations with other customers. I was always disappointed that my knowledge of history and geography was very poor. But here was a way to give me a sense of focus. The other thing is, everything I have ever heard about stamps sticks. Just like when I was a kid and I could remember all the soccer results for four divisions, forty-four games. So it was clear I had a passion for stamps. When I came over here my knowledge of stamps itself had grown so I just did it.

AB: *What exactly is it that draws you to stamp collecting?*

NB: The range of design that goes into stamps is actually staggering. You have the history of graphic design: Art Nouveau, Art Deco, German Expressionism, British Imperialism. So little by little you get involved in "the world." Some people get into the rarity or specifications of a certain stamp, such as where and when it was issued. I would say my interest is a cross between treasure hunting and aesthetics. There is a stamp store here in Vancouver called

Weeders, run by one of the few women in the business. They have a big board with all the bids on it, like an auction. I went in one day and there was a whole sheet valued, but because I know my subject matter really well I recognized this stamp immediately. This was a $300 stamp. I bid on it and got the whole lot for $16.50. It's the sense of having had that treasure hunt, that you've used your superior knowledge combined with observation to make a kill. It's like the primal male hunter.

AB: *You deal with collecting in your latest book,* The Museum at Purgatory, *and seem to argue that what one chooses to collect says something about his personality.*

NB: Everybody collects things. Even people who say they don't may collect shoes, *TV Guides* or whatever. We live in a consumer society, we constantly think that the next purchase will be the one to make us happy. We never learn from the fact that we're disillusioned within 15 seconds of our purchase, and yet we don't look at what those artifacts are. Why are we so crazy to have them? Well, they're mirrors. Take the rock crystal from the book where I scraped it down and added teeth, it's this whole idea of assimilation by proximity. Often when I'm doing a reading I'll talk very seriously and at the end I'll say, "You lot will believe anything, won't you?" Within a relationship, you take on each other's ideas, you take on each other's fluids, and little by little you become part of the other person. That assimilation and oneness is a reality but we, in the West, view things in terms of acute objects, whereas in the East they see change and transition. They would understand the humour in this much better. First you have to prepare the ground before you can tell a joke. Have you ever watched darts? I was in a cinema watching *Carrie*. At one point the three swords of Damocles start swirling around the mother, who's been a nasty piece of work. Then they come diving down and plunge into this woman's chest. Some wanker up front goes, "One hundred and eighty..." and the audience just collapsed. That is the essence of humour. But to understand the joke you need to have watched darts.

AB: *You said that because you came from Britain your sense of humour is different.*

NB: There is more gallows humour but also more surrealism. A woman walks into a butcher shop and asks the butcher, "Have you got a sheep's head?" And the butcher replies, "No Ma'am, that's just the way I part my hair." It's a way of seeing language and thinking about things slightly off centre all the time.

By staying off centre it makes you see the world in your own reality and you don't buy into the collusion of reality that you're being sold. Language is full of self-mockery but we've become so terribly serious.

Matrix *designer Andy Brown interviewed Nick Bantock in his West Vancouver cottage studio on December 14, 1999. It appeared in* Matrix *#57.*

Selected Bibliography

ALLEN, ROBERT

Valhalla at the OK, Ithaca House Press, Ithaca, N.Y., 1971

Blues and Ballads, Ithaca House Press, Ithaca, N.Y., 1974

The Assumption of Private Lives, New Delta Press, Montreal, 1977

The Hawryliw Process, 2 volumes, 1979 & 1981, Porcupine's Quill Press, Erin, Ontario

Wintergarden, Quadrant Editions, Montreal, 1984

One Night at the Indigo Hotel, Cormorant Press, Dunvegan, Ont., 1986

Magellan's Clouds (Selected Poems), Signal Editions, Véhicule Press, Montreal, 1987

A June Night in the Late Cenozoic, Oolichan Books, Lantzville, BC, 1992

Napoleon's Retreat, DC Books, Montreal, 1997

Ricky Ricardo Suites, DC Books, Montreal, 2000

AMIS, MARTIN

Dead Babies, Jonathan Cape, London, 1975

Money, A Suicide Note, Jonathan Cape, London, 1984

Einstein's Monsters, Jonathan Cape, London, 1987

London Fields, Jonathan Cape, London, 1989

Time's Arrow, Jonathan Cape, London, 1991

The Information, Jonathan Cape, London, 1995

Night Train, Jonathan Cape, London, 1997

Heavy Water and Other Stories, Jonathan Cape, London, 1998

BANTOCK, NICK

Fiction:

    Griffin & Sabine, Chronicle Books, San Francisco, 1991

    Sabine's Notebook, Chronicle Books, San Francisco, 1992

    The Golden Mean, Chronicle Books, San Francisco, 1993

    The Egyptian Jukebox, Viking, New York, 1993

    Averse to Beasts, Chronicle Books, San Francisco, 1994

    The Venetian's Wife, Chronicle Books, San Francisco, 1996

    Paris Out of Hand, Chronicle Books, San Francisco, 1996 (Collaboration of
        Nick Bantock, Karen Elizabeth Gordon, and Barbara Hodgson)

    The Forgetting Room, HarperCollins, New York, 1997

    The Museum at Purgatory, HarperCollins, 1999

    The Artful Dodger, Chronicle & Raincoast Books, San Francisco & Vancouver, 2C

Pop-ups:

    There Was An Old Lady, Viking, New York, 1990

    Wings, Random House, New York, 1990

    Jabberwocky, Viking, New York, 1991

    Solomon Grundy, Viking, New York, 1992

    The Walrus and The Carpenter, Viking, New York, 1992

    Runners, Sliders, Bouncers, Climbers, Hyperion, 1992

    Robin Hood, Viking, New York, 1993

CD ROM:

    Ceremony of Innocence, Real World, U.K., 1997

Others:

    The Missing Nose Flute, Chronicle Books, San Francisco, 1991

    Capolan ArtBox, Chronicle Books, San Francisco, 1997

BLAIS, MARIE-CLAIRE

    Mad Shadows, Jonathan Cape, New York, 1960
        (Translated by Merloyd Lawrence)

    A Season in the Life of Emmanuel, Farrar Strauss Giroux, New York, 1966

    The Manuscripts of Pauline Archange, Farrar Strauss Girous, New York, 1970

    St. Lawrence Blues, Doubleday Canada, Toronto, 1973
        (Translated by Ralph Manheim)

The Execution, Talonbooks, Vancouver, 1976
Deaf to the City, Lester Orpen Denys, Toronto, 1981
　　　(Translated by Carol Dunlop)
Veiled Countries/Lives, Signal Editions, Véhicule Press, Montreal, 1984
　　　(Translated by Michael Harris)
Pierre, Acropole, Paris, 1986
The Angel of Solitude, Talonbooks, Vancouver, 1993
American Notebooks: A Writer's Journey, Talonbooks, Vancouver, 1996

BISSOONDATH, NEIL

Digging up the Mountains, Macmillan, Toronto, 1985
A Casual Brutality, Macmillan, Toronto, 1988
On the Eve of Uncertain Tomorrows, Lester and Orpen Dennys,
　　　Toronto, 1990
Selling Illusions: The Cult of Multiculturalism in Canada, Penguin, Toronto, 19
The Innocence of Age, Knopf, New York, 1992
The Worlds Within Her, 1999

BOLSTER, STEPHANIE

White Stone: The Alice Poems, Signal Editions, Véhicule Press,
　　　Montreal, Qc., 1998
Two Bowls of Milk, McClelland and Stewart, Toronto, 1999

CARSON, ANNE

Eros the Bittersweet, Princeton UP, Princeton, NJ, 1986
Short Talks, Brick Books, Toronto, 1992
Glass, Irony and God, New Directions, New York, 1995
Plainwater: Essays and Poetry, Knopf, New York, 1995
Autobiography of Red, Knopf, New York, 1998
Economy of the Unlost, Princeton UP, Princeton, NJ, 1999
The Beauty of the Husband: A Fictional Essay in 29 Tangos, Knopf,
　　　New York, 2001

CRUMMEY, MICHAEL

Arguments with Gravity, Quarry Press, Kingston, Ontario, 1996
Flesh and Blood, Beach Holme Books, Vancouver, 1998
Hard Light, Brick Books, London, Ont., 1998
Emergency Roadside Assistance, Trout Lily Press, 2001

FENNARIO, DAVID

Without a Parachute, McClelland and Stewart, Toronto, 1972
On the Job, Talonbooks, Vancouver, 1976
Nothing to Lose, Talonbooks, Vancouver, 1977
Balconville, Talonbooks, Vancouver, 1980
Blue Mondays, Black Rock Creations, Montreal, 1984
Joe Beef, A History of Pointe St. Charles , Talonbooks, Vancouver, 1990
Doctor Thomas Neill Cream, Mystery of McGill , Talonbooks, Vancouver, 1994

GHOSH, AMITAV

The Glass Palace, Hamish Hamilton, London, 1986
The Shadowlines, Vavi Dayal, New Delhi, 1988
In an Antique Land, Granta, London, 1992
The Calcutta Chromosome: A Novel of Fevers, Delirium, and Discovery
        Knopf, New York, 1995
Dancing in Calcutta, Ravi Dayal, New Delhi, 1998

HARRIS, MICHAEL

Sparks, New Delta Press, Montreal, 1976
Grace, New Delta Press, Montreal, 1977
Miss Emily et la Mort, VLB Editeur, Montreal, 1984
In Transit, Signal Editions, Véhicule Press, Montreal, 1985
New and Selected Poems, Signal Editions, Véhicule Press, Montreal, 1994

JONES, D. G.

Frost on the Sun, Contact Press, Montreal/Toronto, 1957
The Sun is Axeman, University of Toronto Press, Toronto, 1961
Butterfly on Rock, University of Toronto Press, Toronto, 1970
Under the Thunder the Flowers Light up the Earth, Coach House Press,
    Toronto, 1977
A Throw of Particles: New and Selected Poems of D. G. Jones,
    General Publishing, Toronto, 1983
Balthazar and Other Poems, Coach House Press, Toronto, 1988
The Floating Garden, Coach House Press, Toronto, 1995
Wild Asterisks in Cloud, Empyreal Editions, Montreal, 1997

LAYTON, IRVING

The Swinging Flesh, McClelland and Stewart, Toronto, 1961
Love Where the Nights are Long (ed.), McClelland and Stewart,
    Toronto, 1962
Periods of the Moon, McClelland and Stewart, Toronto, 1967
The Shattered Plinths, McClelland and Stewart, Toronto, 1968
Selected Poems, McClelland and Stewart, Toronto, 1969
The Whole Bloody Bird, McClelland and Stewart, Toronto, 1969
The Collected Poems of Irving Layton, McClelland and Stewart,
    Toronto, 1971
Engagements: The Prose of Irving Layton, McClelland and Stewart,
    Toronto, 1972
Lovers and Lesser Men, McClelland & Stewart, Toronto, 1972
The pole-vaulter, McClelland & Stewart, Toronto, 1974
For my brother Jesus, McClelland and Stewart, Toronto, 1976
The selected poems of Irving Layton, Edited by Eli Mandel; with an introd.
    by Hugh Kenner, New Directions Pub. Corp., New York, 1977
The Covenant, McClelland and Stewart, Toronto, 1977
The Tightrope Dancer, McClelland and Stewart, Toronto, 1978
Droppings From Heaven, McClelland and Stewart, Toronto, 1979
For My Neighbours In Hell, Mosaic Press, Oakville, Ont., 1980
A Wild Peculiar Joy: Selected Poems, 1945-82. McClelland and Stewart,
    Toronto, 1982
The Gucci Bag, Mosaic Press, Oakville, Ont., 1983

The Love Poems of Irving Layton: With Reverence & Delight. Mosaic
Press, Oakville, Ont., 1984
Final Reckoning: Poems, 1982-1986, Mosaic Press, Oakville, Ont., 1987
Dance With Desire: Selected Love Poems, Drawings by Richard Gorman,
Porcupine's Quill, Erin, Ont., 1992

MAJZELS, ROBERT

The Guerilla is like a Poet, Cormorant Press, Dunvegan, Ont., 1988
Hellman's Scrapbook, Cormorant Press, Dunvegan, Ont., 1992
City of Forgetting, Mercury Press, Toronto, Ont., 1997

MOURÉ, ERIN

Empire, York St., Anansi, Toronto, 1979
The Whiskey Vigil, Harbour Publishing, Madeira Park, B.C., 1981
Wanted Alive, Anansi, Toronto, 1983
Furious, Anansi, Toronto, 1988
WSW, Véhicule Press, Montreal, 1989
The Green Word: Selected Poems, 1973-92, Oxford Univ. Press, 1994
Search Procedures, Anansi, Toronto, 1996
A Frame of the Book, Anansi, Toronto, 1999
Sheep's Vigil by a Fervent Person, Anansi, Toronto, 2001

SCOTT, GAIL

Spare Parts, Coach House Press, Toronto, 1981
Heroine, Coach House Press, Toronto, 1987
Spaces Like Stairs, Women's Press, Toronto, 1989
Main Brides, Coach House Press, Toronto, 1993
My Paris, Mercury Press, Toronto, 1999

Acknowledgements

Thanks for permission to reprint to all the interviewers herein. Thanks also to Meghan Hicks, Kristine Kaposy, Nancy Saunders, and Melissa Thompson for editorial help.

Cover Photo Credits (where known):